Royal Red

A Cozy Fantasy Adventure

K.C. Shaw

STRANGE ANIMAL PUBLISHING

Cover art by Kial F. 'CynicalStith'

Contents

Important Author's Note

Even though this book has a pink dragon on the cover and is about a dragon artist and her adventures, it's also not for kids.

The dragons in this book are adults. There's bad language and one explicit sex scene.

On the plus side, the sex is consensual and presented positively. But it's still not for kids.

One

Rose spent all afternoon staring at the rain and dabbing paint on her new canvas. She liked the view from her bedroom, which overlooked the cobbled road between Riverside Artists' Cooperative and Gallery and a couple of small shops. The shops had cheerful striped awnings that contrasted beautifully with the gray day. Rose tried to convey the juxtaposition, but the more she worked, the more amateurish her results were.

After three hours the rain stopped and she gave up, cleaned her brushes, and went downstairs to the co-op's kitchen.

Honey had set her own easel by the kitchen's big window. She was in the way, but it was her building and she had started the co-op, so if she wanted to block the entrance and fill the kitchen with turpentine fumes while other dragons were trying to eat, no one would complain. Not to her face, anyway. Rose stepped over Honey's tail and settled at the big table.

Because Rose's room was directly above the kitchen, Honey was painting nearly the same view Rose had failed to capture. The canvas upstairs was a blurry mess of grays and blues that looked more like molten lead than rain. Honey's canvas shone with vibrant colors that invoked the rain-washed street.

Rose picked at the bowl of dried liver someone had left out. Honey made it look so *easy*.

"There." Honey shuffled back without getting to her feet. "I think it's done. What do you think?"

"It's perfect." Rose sighed. "I tried to paint the rain too and it's just a mess. How do you do it?"

Honey wiped her brushes on a paint-stained rag. "First you practice for fifty years, more or less. It'll come, Rose."

"Really? Because I don't seem to be making any progress lately."

"Try something new. Try a different approach. Get a traveling kit and fly somewhere—different views, different skies. You stay up in that room too much."

Rose paused with a piece of liver halfway to her mouth and thought about different skies. How odd that Honey would put it that way—but how exact. Just like the dabs of bright white in her painting that suggested light shining off puddles.

Different skies, new horizons. She'd always been a good flyer, had even been on the team in school. Artists often traveled to keep from getting stale. It would do her good.

Honey finished with her brushes and scrubbed paint from her paws with a rag. Her soft gold-brown hide gleamed in the light streaming through the window. "Who's cooking tonight?"

Rose tossed the liver back into the bowl. "Who cares? Honey, I'm going to travel the world!"

Of course it wasn't that simple, not once Rose thought it over. It was still winter, rainy and chilly. Besides, she needed supplies and more money.

She discussed it with the others while they ate—elk stew with carrots, made by May, who was the only one in the co-op who could really cook.

"It's exciting." Elm was the biggest dragon Rose knew, and his mottled green-brown hide made him look like something that lived under a hedge. He ate hunched over with his tail curled around his feet like a cat. "We ought to hold an exhibit of your stuff before you go."

"I need to get some canvases done first." Rose sopped up the last of the broth in her bowl with a hunk of bread.

Honey said, "Do a series of pre-travel pieces. We'll drum up interest by telling everyone they're the last pieces you'll have available for—how long?"

"I don't know. Spring and summer at least."

"Say six months. That sounds like a good long time."

"You could have a baby in six months," Blossom said, and laughed. "Will you fool around?"

Rose thought the question was in poor taste. She just said, "I need to buy a travel kit and fly to different places nearby to paint, get back flying fit."

"Good idea," Honey said. "You can have my old kit if you like. I never use it anymore."

"Really?" Rose forgave Honey for painting in the kitchen. "I'll be careful with it."

"Use it, that's all I ask."

Blossom, predictably, didn't let the thread of her thoughts drop. "It wouldn't be that fun to fool around while you're traveling, actually. Not unless he went with you. You'd have to wait out your egg months without him, and what if you found someone more interesting in the meantime?"

May, a pretty pink with brown dapples, said, "It could be awfully romantic, though. Think of it, Rose. He sees you in an exotic marketplace and falls for your beauty. You spurn him, he pursues you across the country, groveling—"

"How will he grovel while flying," Blossom said, "and why would Rose spurn him?"

"Because he's plain, but he has a heart of gold. Finally he wins your heart and the two of you join in love, twined together under the full moon—"

"*May*," Rose said, horrified. She couldn't look at Sable, who was sitting right next to her. "Do you mind?"

"But if it's a pure love and true, there's no shame," May said, eyes wide. You couldn't argue with her, that was the problem.

Rose grabbed more bread. "I'm going abroad to paint. I will not be twining about with anyone."

"In the *moonlight*," Blossom said, drawing out the word until it sounded filthy.

"Shut up, Blossom. You started this," Rose said.

May cocked her head, a birdlike trait that would look contrived on just about anyone else. "Well, it would be awkward to have an egg somewhere foreign. Who knows what their nurseries are like? And if you wanted to keep the baby, of course you'd be stuck another month until the egg hatched and you could bundle it up and fly home with it."

Rose discovered she had mashed the hunk of bread in her paw until it resembled dough. "I am *not* going to have an egg, don't be absurd. I'm going to paint and paint and paint. Honey, can I look at your travel kit? I want to gloat over it."

Honey ducked her head in a nod, an amused twinkle in her amber eyes. "Yes, come up with me and help me find it."

Rose spent the evening packing and repacking her paints and brushes into the travel kit. The rain blew off, revealing a starry night sky that promised a glorious winter's morning to follow. She had trouble sleeping.

She woke just before dawn, packed the kit again with a small fresh canvas, and strapped it on. It buckled around her waist, just behind where her wing leathers attached to her sides, which meant the kit itself snugged against her lower belly. She tried to adjust it higher but it wouldn't go. She would just have to get used to it.

The eastern sky blushed pink as she leaped from her window. She stretched her wings and felt them cup the air with every powerful downbeat. She felt invincible.

She flew above the buildings and roads of Whitefall. Elk-drawn wagons made deliveries far below, and the first commuters flew from home to office with lunch sacks dangling from claws. Rose coasted over the broad flat roof of the city's nursery and then she was above farms and pastures.

She flew on and on as the sun rose. Farmland gave way to forest; here and there a road or stream snaked through the trees. She flew above the village of Foxbury, rustic and charming from above, and angled her wings to descend.

Rose had only been to Foxbury a few times, but she remembered a humped stone bridge that crossed a narrow river. It would be a good subject to paint. People liked that sort of thing and it would sell if she did a halfway decent job.

The sun was well up by the time she dropped to her feet in the town square. As always after flying any distance, her first steps felt clumsy and slow.

Her wing muscles trembled with such unexpected exertion. Her mouth was parched, she was starving, and the thought of the flight home filled her with dismay.

She stepped into a café and bought tea and ham rolls. They were so good she stayed in the café for the next hour, sipping tea from a porcelain bowl and sketching the view from the window.

She returned home late, a decent but uninspired painting in the travel kit. She dumped the kit in the corner, burrowed into her nest of blankets, and fell asleep almost immediately.

In the morning she was so sore she could barely make the short flight to the nearest bakery. She walked back with the bag of pastries held in her teeth.

Honey met her in the kitchen. "Tired?"

Rose dropped the bag on the table. "Worn out. I think I might have been a little too ambitious."

"What did you paint?"

"Foxbury's bridge. I'll show you."

Rose trotted upstairs and retrieved her canvas, the oil paint still gleaming wetly. It wasn't bad. Nothing to be ashamed of, yet for some reason she was.

Honey examined it for several minutes without comment. Rose tried not to squirm. Finally the older dragon said, "It'll sell, of course. Quite a nice subject and you chose a good angle. You do a good job with light; that water looks real."

Rose didn't respond. She knew what was coming next.

Honey continued, "It's boring, though—a safe painting. Even your brushstrokes are safe. You control the brush so carefully the brushstrokes are short and cautious."

"I've never been good at painting quickly," Rose said. "I never like the results."

"Perhaps you haven't tried often enough. Next time you go out, make the sky your subject. Bring several canvases and paint as fast as you can."

"All right." Rose stared at her safe painting and felt like a hack, a greeting card artist. Even Elm, who specialized in saccharine studies of eggs, had a genius way with light and shadow that lifted his work above its subject.

"I'll do better," Rose said, and wondered if she could.

The next day was Rose's day in the shop. She was secretly glad, although she complained about it at breakfast. "I wanted to fly today. I'm going to do some sky studies."

May cocked her head. "Just the sky or a landscape too?"

"Just the sky, I think."

"You should paint the sunrise. I've never been able to get it right, myself."

Despite May's cutesy mannerisms and wide-eyed innocence that sometimes verged on disingenuousness, her paintings were dark, ferocious, and beautiful. Rose sometimes wondered at the contrast. As far as she could tell, May's only goal in life was to get into the city's breeding program—yet she clearly had hidden depths or she could not paint as she did.

Sable speared a piece of ham on a claw and contemplated it as though he'd never seen ham before. "Paint a storm."

May said, "The rain would ruin her canvas."

"Well, I can't do anything today," Rose said. She ducked her head to glare at Sable. "Don't play with your food."

He saluted her with the ham and crammed it into his mouth all at once. May giggled. Honey yawned.

The weather was fine and they had new paintings in the gallery, so a number of dragons stopped in to browse. A young couple, the female so round Rose worried she would lay her egg in the middle of the shop, spent an hour picking out a painting for their new house. The male wanted one of Elm's more treacly paintings, of a sleeping dragon curled around her pearly egg; the female admired May's latest, a dragon either swimming or drowning in a turbulent river. Both expressed horror at Sable's display.

Rose finally said, "We offer a ten percent discount if you buy more than one painting," and they bought both.

When they had gone, Rose went around the shop herself and examined each piece that showed the sky. Honey's skies were quick dabs and blobs of paint, gray and white and blue. Elm's were super-realistic, with clouds lit as though from within. May's were slashes of color that suggested the sky without being particularly sky-like—Rose wondered how May knew she could not paint the sunrise. Maybe she had only been making conversation. Blossom's paintings were mostly claustrophobic interior pieces; her only skies were slices of blue or gray glimpsed through windows.

Only one of Sable's pieces showed the sky, and of course it was a churning mass of storm clouds. An abandoned egg lay in the foreground, beaded with rain. Just looking at it made Rose anxious. That was the point of Sable's paintings, of course. He liked to disturb and horrify the viewer. He rarely painted dragons, only eggs: eggs abandoned, cracked, smashed, or in some sort of peril. His gallery showings were always packed with dragons who wanted to glimpse the notorious artist, and Sable lurked in the background looking dangerous and saturnine. People wrote angry letters to the papers about him. Yet Sable was kind, never bragged about being in the breeding program, and was always the first to help out with any bothersome chore.

People were strange. Artists were strange. And Rose could not think of Sable without longing in her belly, which was embarrassing since he wasn't interested in her.

The next day she made herself fly to the hills south of Whitefall. She found a hill remote enough that she could paint in peace, unpacked her kit, and looked up at the sky to decide what colors she needed for her palette.

It was a windy day and clouds were moving in fast. It would probably rain by evening. Rose stared at the clouds, noting the way they changed and moved. She studied the colors of the sky, the way light pierced the clouds and shone on the hillsides below. She sniffed the wind. When it grew chilly she wrapped her wings tightly around herself.

The morning drew on. Rose ate her roast elk sandwich and drank her flask of water. Clouds covered the sky and they were different than before, so she continued to watch them. Occasionally she picked up a tube of paint but always put it back down.

Late afternoon brought the first spit of rain. Rose packed up the kit without having painted a single stroke, and flew home.

She felt it had been a productive day.

She dreamed of clouds that night. When she woke at dawn, she grabbed the travel kit before she even visited the latrine.

She flew to the same hill as before, but this time she didn't hesitate. She prepared her palette so quickly she lost the cap of one of her paint tubes in the grass. She screwed a piece of paper over the opening to keep the paint from getting everywhere. Then she selected a wide flat brush—different from her usual favorites—and looked up at the sky.

Dawn was not far advanced. Flat-bottomed clouds shone pink and gold against the dark western sky, while the eastern sky glowed with sunrise. The scene changed from moment to moment as the light grew.

Honey was right. Rose could not paint the sky in her usual manner. It was not a rustic bridge or a rainy street that would stay put while she made each meticulous stroke.

She jabbed her brush into the blue with short, nervous motions, dragged a little white into it, a touch of yellow.

She painted.

Fifteen minutes later she blinked and drew back from the canvas. She was breathing so hard she might have been flying instead of painting. The canvas was a sky—not perfect, certainly not her usual clean look, but energetic, atmospheric, and undeniably a sunrise.

She had brought another canvas, but she packed everything away carefully and returned home in time for breakfast.

"Back already?" Honey glanced up from chopping an apple.

"Yes. What do you think?" Rose unbuckled the travel kit and opened it to reveal the painting clipped in place.

Honey abandoned the apple, the bacon blackening in the pan. She looked at the painting closely, then stepped back to look again. Rose tried not to fidget.

Finally Honey said, "It's very, very good. Well done, Rose. I knew you had it in you."

Rose slumped to the floor in pretend exhaustion. "Thank goodness."

"The hard part will be keeping up that looser style. You'll need to practice until it's second nature."

Sable wandered into the kitchen, his golden eyes half-lidded against the morning light. "The bacon's burning. Who painted this? You, Rose?"

Rose scrambled to her feet, embarrassed. "Yes. This morning. Don't touch it."

"Of course not," Sable said, and Rose was embarrassed again. Sable knew better than to touch a fresh painting. "I like it. Not your usual style."

"I'm trying to branch out. That's the whole point of traveling."

"Maybe you won't need to travel after all."

Behind them, rescuing the bacon, Honey said, "It's important to follow through on these things," as though she knew Rose was already regretting her decision.

Rose fell into the habit of flying every morning. It was a chore at first as her body protested the sudden activity after years of indolence. Soon, though, she found she missed her dawn flight if she had to skip it.

She lost the chubbiness around her middle that had bothered her for months. She could gallop up the stairs without puffing. By the time the silverbirds returned, heralding early spring, Rose could fly for hours without tiring or feeling battered the next day.

Painting was more difficult. For two weeks she painted nothing but skyscapes, at least one a day. Three of them Honey judged good enough to put in the shop, one Rose liked so much she matted it and hung it in her room. But when she tried to use the new fast style for painting anything else, she ended up with an amateurish mess.

"Don't try figures yet," Honey said. "Trees. Individual trees, forests, things like that. See what you can do with them."

Feeling as though she was back in school, with the old dread of inadequacy, Rose painted trees.

They bored her. They did not change like the sky, just sat there. Her paintings were lifeless. Honey made suggestions but nothing Rose tried made a difference.

She was trying to paint the cedar in the co-op's small weedy yard one afternoon when Sable stole up behind her. He moved so quietly that Rose didn't even know he was there until he said, "You might make it look menacing."

Rose jumped and dropped her brush. "You scared me!"

"Sorry. That tree's menacing. See how dark it is and the way its branches are crooked like claws?"

"Not really. It's just a tree," Rose said, sullen from being startled and unable, as always, to say the right thing when talking to Sable.

"If you think that way, you'll never be able to paint it—or anything else."

Rose wilted inside at his quick dismissal of her abilities, even while she agreed with him. "How would you do it, then?" she said with ill grace.

Sable nudged her aside, sending her stomach fluttering. He smelled musky in the warm afternoon. Sunlight slanted into the yard, making everything bright and flat with hard-edged shadows. Sable's black hide gleamed with iridescence like a crow's back.

He painted over her uninspired mess. With his attention focused on the canvas and the stupid tree, Rose looked him over without fear of him noticing. He was more fit than she remembered and she wondered if he too had been flying. The black horns arching back from his head gleamed with oil.

"Here, see? The tree has a personality if you give it one. It's not just a tree."

Rose stopped admiring the muscular curve of Sable's haunches as he crouched at the easel. His painting was only roughed in—his usual style was deliberate and it usually took him weeks to get a piece the way he wanted it—but even so, the cedar brooded on the canvas. It had presence.

"It's good." Rose looked away. She would never get it right. Worse, she suspected she could not go back to her old style of painting. She would never be able to paint anything but skies.

Sable put the paintbrush in her paw and curled her fingers around it, his own fingers warm on hers. Her heart hammered. "Now you try. Want a clean canvas?"

"Yes. I brought some. I mean, they're in my room but I meant to bring them—I'll get one."

"I'll get it. Be right back."

His wings nearly buffeted her as he sprang into the air. She felt the power of the leap, saw the dead leaves fly from his first down-stroke. She stared after him.

Flirting. He was flirting with her. With *her*.

He returned a moment later and set the fresh canvas on the easel. "Go."

She looked at the tree without seeing it. Sable was flirting with her. Sable was in the breeding program and was called on to mate at *least* once a month with some of the most beautiful females in Whitefall. And he was flirting with her.

Light shone on the cedar, which turned it into shadow with barely a gleam on its spiny needles. The bark was scaly and the whole tree bristled.

Sable saw menace, but Sable saw menace everywhere. Rose noticed the patches of light and shadow in the tree's dark greenery. It reminded her of the patchiness of clouds in bright sunlight.

She jabbed at the palette. Green, blue to deepen the green, a little yellow to highlight; a slash of red in the branches, nearly hidden in the muddier shades of brown. Funny she had never noticed how much like clouds tree branches were. Only the colors were different.

She stopped and looked at what she'd painted. The tree had come to life in less than ten minutes—still an unfinished canvas, since she had not bothered with a background, but as vibrant as her previous attempts had been dead.

Sable stared from the painting to her and back. Rose swallowed.

"You are very talented," he said quietly. Then he stood and flew away.

"Thank you," Rose said, although he was already too far away to hear.

Two

For the next week Rose did nothing but paint and fly, fly and paint. Blossom took her shop day, an unusually kind gesture until she said that evening at supper, "Of course you'll take one of my days before you leave."

"When are you leaving?" May asked.

Rose admired the colors of the food in her bowl: pink ham, ˙ow and brown cornbread, green beans. "Mm? I don't know. I ˙'t decided yet." Her dinner would make a good still-life. She ning low on canvases; she would need to gesso over some ˙nes.

˙ better be soon?" Blossom said. "Someone make her her eat or she'll stare at her food all night."

˙e to stop Blossom from commenting further. "Af-

˙ Honey poured herself more water from the

know." Rose wanted to stay home and ew paintings were selling much faster

"Maybe I should stay after all," she said to Honey the next morning. Honey was an early riser and Rose had become one so she could paint the dawn clouds as often as possible.

The morning was overcast and windy. Honey was setting up her easel in the kitchen to paint the coming rain, but she stopped and turned to Rose. "No. You're not done."

"But—my new style."

"You've taken a jump in the right direction but you're *not* done. What you're doing now is good, sometimes very good, but you still have to find your depth."

"I can do that here." Rose fidgeted her tail against the flagstone floor, an old habit she had broken years ago. She thought of Sable, who had been avoiding her all week. She wanted him to keep flirting with her. She didn't want to leave.

Honey drew herself up and arched her neck. Rose crouched down automatically, cringing in apology like a hatchling caught doing mischief. "Finish what you start."

"Yes. All right. I'll buy a guide book." Rose slunk out of the kitchen.

She seethed as she flew across town. Honey wasn't Rose's mother. She should leave the co-op, found one of her own across town and become a rival. That would show Honey who had depth.

"Rose! Slow down!"

Rose backwinged and turned her head to look behind her. May was thrashing through the air, jaws open as she panted.

"Sorry, I didn't know you were following me," Rose said when May caught up.

"I saw you leave and thought I'd join you, but you're so *fast*." May's pale hide shone in the dawn light. "Where are you going?"

"To buy a guide book and a map."

"You've already passed the nearest book store."

"I thought I'd go to the excursion shop near the river." Rose had only just thought of it, but it seemed like a good idea after all. "I need a pack."

"It's so exciting! I'd like to travel, but if you leave Dayrill they won't consider you for the breeding program for a full year after you come back. That's what Sable said, anyway."

The river came into view, curving through the low hills. The streets below were blurry with fog. Rose and May banked and circled to lose height, then dropped to the street.

The fog beaded Rose's hide with moisture, which made her itch. She rubbed her sides with her wings.

"Ugh, I'm starting to molt already," May said.

"Me too." Rose pushed through the double leather flaps across the doorway and entered the shop.

The tables inside were heaped with goods. Old maps papered the walls, which gave the shop a musty bookish smell. Rose looked around and felt her interest spark.

"There are packs over here," May said. "What sort are you looking for?"

Rose followed her to the trestle tables. "Something big enough to hold the kit Honey gave me."

"These are on sale."

A mottled brown and white male joined them. "You're looking for a backpack? We've got some new ones over here. This is my favorite type; I have one like it."

May giggled and glanced sideways at the clerk. He was attractive, Rose had to admit—lithe and muscular—but she thought of Sable and there was no comparison.

The clerk showed her how to fit one arm through the loop, then settle the pack between her wings before putting the other arm loop on. "Let me load some books in it so you can see what it feels like full. What do you think?"

"It's comfortable." Rose sat back on her haunches and flapped her wings, stirring the maps pinned to the walls. The pack stayed put, and the arm loops were supple rolled leather that would not chafe. "Let me look at some of the other ones before I make a decision."

She ended up buying the pack, along with a guide book to the Southern Lands and a detailed vellum map. Rolled up, the map fit neatly into a pocket built into her new pack.

"Where are you traveling?" the clerk asked before she left.

"Everywhere."

The backpack excited everyone. It was too small for Elm even after Rose let the straps out all the way, but everyone else tried it on in the yard.

Honey stretched her wings and shook them with a leathery slapping sound. "Very comfortable. I wish I'd had something like this when I was your age."

"You traveled?" Rose said.

"Three months along the Stekkan Mountains. I thought you knew." Honey took the pack off and handed it to Blossom, who wriggled into it. "I went with two friends, Amber Whitetail and Oriole Sky. We sold paintings as we went to pay our way."

"Oriole Sky! I've heard of her," Blossom said, looking up from adjusting a buckle.

"Oh yes, she got quite famous for a while. She's fallen a bit out of favor but she's very good. You should visit her, Rose. She met a male in North Stekka and stayed with him. Amber and I continued our travels but Oriole is still in North Stekka as far as I know, still painting the same mountains."

Sable turned his head sharply to look at Rose. She pretended she didn't notice. "I'd love to meet her."

"I'll send a letter of introduction with you. I can't remember her mate's name, and we fell out of conversing years ago. I know they had children but of course they'd be grown now. I can't believe it's been so long." Honey stared into the sky as though looking at something else entirely. Her hide looked dull in the sunlight.

May said, "Perhaps you'll find a mate while you're gone, Rose."

Sable was still staring at her. Rose still didn't look, although she felt he was drilling holes through her with the intensity of his gaze. "I'm not looking for a mate. I just want to improve my painting and see the world."

"That's what Oriole said too." Honey sat down and scratched her side with a hind foot like a dog. "Ugh, I'm molting."

"It's the heat," Elm said. "Early spring, early molt."

Blossom leaped into the air, sending dead leaves flying. She circled the cedar twice and thumped back down, slightly winded. "I like it. Maybe I'll go with you."

Rose could not think of a dragon she wanted to travel with *less* than Blossom. "You'd need to get fit in the next month, if you can," she said unkindly.

Blossom laughed. "Not likely. Try it on, May."

"The straps will make me itch."

"Itch now, itch later—we all itch during molt," Blossom said.

"Itch and bitch," Elm said, and everyone laughed.

Elm was right, although really spring was no warmer or earlier than usual. Within three days they were all scratching and complaining.

No one got any real work done and the shop had almost no customers. The papers were full of the usual advice, from sandbathing to drinking extra water; every store put up big signs advertising anti-itch oils and creams. Nothing helped.

Rose had to make herself go out for her morning flight. Doing anything during molt was awful, even eating, although once she was in the air she felt better. Landing was another thing. All the itching she did not feel with the wind rushing over her hide returned with a vengeance once she was on the ground.

On the fifth full day of molt, when the misery was at its peak and no one was even pretending to be nice anymore, Rose decided to fly all day. She forced down a few mouthfuls of meat gruel, then launched herself out the kitchen door. It was raining.

Seven hours later she returned, her wings so tired she let them drag on the floor once she landed. She had flown directly into her own room, intending to drop onto her blanket and rest. But she needed food first.

By the time she was halfway down the steps, the itching reached such an unbearable pitch Rose wondered if she would actually die. She heard a stream of muttered swearing from Elm's room as she passed it, a few despairing whimpers from Blossom's.

May was in the kitchen. She'd tied a white dishcloth around her muzzle like the Silent Nurses who thought infection was carried on the breath. She was sweeping up drifts of molted scales, but stopped and stared when Rose came in.

Rose stared back. May's usual freckled hide was grayish, with molting hide hanging in shreds. Her gold eyes were round and frantic with misery above the dishcloth.

Rose's own hide was beaded with rain, which made her look slightly less awful. She tried to fold her wings and had no energy to do so. Every inch of her body was an endless agony of itching—an itch no scratch could satisfy, an itch that killed appetite and murdered sleep.

Her half-eaten bowl of gruel sat where she had left it that morning. It had congealed into a rancid-looking brown mass.

Rose ate it anyway, gagging it down all at once. She looked at May, still staring, and gave a wordless, birdlike screech. Then she dragged herself upstairs to her room.

Three

Gradually the itching abated. Last year's dead scales shed in earnest, revealing patches of lovely new hide. Rose no longer dreaded stopping flying. Elm and Honey cleaned the kitchen, and Rose went shopping and brought the groceries back in her pack. It was so nicely balanced she scarcely noticed the extra weight.

The newspapers proclaimed in huge letters, as they did every year, "IT'S OVER!" Sable emerged from his room for the first time in almost two weeks. Rose supposed he must come out sometimes, if only to use the latrine, but if so he made sure no one was around.

They all had lunch together outside: half a roast elk that Honey had ordered delivered that morning to celebrate. They lay it on a cheery green oilcloth and gathered around it to gorge themselves like vultures. Daffodils and white illil flowers bloomed along the edges of the yard, birds sang, and the sun gleamed on clean new hide and crisp markings.

"We all look very fine," Honey said when everyone's hunger was sated and the elk was reduced nearly to bones. "It's worth the itching."

"You say that every year, and every year I disagree," Elm said. "I look the same anyway."

"You're gorgeous," May said, and made a show of looking him over. Elm arched his neck and gave her a flirty glance from the corner of his eye. Blossom snickered.

The mail arrived—newspapers and the small blue envelopes the breeding council used, summoning Sable to his breeding appointments. There were a lot of them this time, enough that he shuffled them into a little pile and sat on them with an embarrassed glance at Rose.

Blossom grabbed one of the newspapers. "Keeping you busy, aren't they?" she said to Sable. "You won't have the energy to mate with anyone of your own choosing."

"I always have enough energy."

Rose pretended she had not heard the exchange, but inside she seethed. Trust Blossom to make a play for Sable during the one time of year he would find her interesting.

Not that Rose wanted to start her traveling on a mating restriction. The restriction had recently been lowered to seven weeks from eight—amid huge controversy—but it was still a long time to wait between partners. It would be different if she was staying home, of course. She and Sable could be together as often as they liked. But she didn't want to wait seven weeks during her travels. She might meet a fascinating male and have to tell him no.

She didn't intend to look for a male on her travels. But she wanted it to be a possibility, although she would not admit it to anyone.

Honey said, "There's unrest in South Stekka, Rose. Are you going there?"

"I haven't decided. What sort of unrest?"

Honey folded the newspaper page back and read aloud. "'A royalist movement in Sather has caused upheaval in recent months. Elected officials have received threats and several public buildings have been damaged by fire. Rumors that the hatchery will be targeted next has caused panic and near riots, with hatchery guards being demanded.'"

"I'll try not to be elected to office while I'm in South Stekka," Rose said.

"Maybe they'll make you their queen, like in the olden days," May said. "You'll come home wearing a golden chain."

Elm had taken part of Blossom's paper. "The *Detail* is predicting a record number of new year babies this year. They're running a contest. If you guess the number of eggs laid three months from now, you can win a chicken a day for a whole year."

"I don't want to eat nothing but chicken for a whole year," May said.

Blossom shook the page she was reading. "Forget chicken, I've found the best article ever written. 'Please Your Mate with a Novel Position.'"

Honey laughed. Rose said, "The *Detail* is obsessed with sex."

"Aren't we all?" Elm shrugged his wings.

Blossom said, "There are drawings and everything. Rather good artwork, actually. It doesn't say who did it."

They crowded around to look at the drawings. They were good, and definitely arousing. May said, "They ought not to put those in the paper. It's coarse. Ooh, look at that one. You'd have to be awfully limber."

Honey said, "Clear skies, that makes even me want to go to the fair."

"You're not that old," Rose said. "You ought to go. Find yourself a handsome new year's stud."

"Maybe." Honey stepped over Sable's tail. "I thought the council capped males at six a month. You've got seven envelopes here."

Sable gathered up the little envelopes and sat on them again. "I'll look at them later."

"Check them now. If they've overbooked you, you need to let them know right away."

Sable muttered something that sounded like "Bossy," but he flipped through the envelopes. "Oh. This one's not mine."

"Better fly it to the post office so they can get it to the right dragon," Honey said.

"No, it's May's."

He handed the envelope to May, who gave a little gasp of excitement. "It might be a no again," she said, "but those come in white envelopes."

"Open it!" Blossom shouted.

May did. "Oh! Oh, oh, oh, they want me on a trial basis this year! My first appointment is next week."

"Congratulations," Rose said with as much warmth as she could muster, even though she couldn't imagine wanting to be in the breeding program. But May was clearly overjoyed.

Blossom said, "How awkward if your first appointment was with Sable."

Sable scrambled to open all his envelopes so he could compare appointment times with May. "No match. Not that I wouldn't be delighted, of course," he said with a courtly nod.

Only Elm didn't seem particularly enthusiastic about May's triumph. It must be hard on him, Rose thought, to almost have her only to find her snatched away at the last moment. He would have to visit the fair himself for new year's, unless he intended to make himself miserable by abstaining.

Blossom waited until a lull in the conversation to announce, "The breeding program is an antiquated relic of a stratified society. It should be banned."

They all looked at her, startled. May said, "Anyone can apply these days." She sounded hurt.

Elm said, with as much anger as he ever showed, "Where did you memorize that, Blossom? There wasn't a single 'fuck' in the whole sentence."

Everyone snickered, even Blossom. Honey pointedly changed the subject.

Later, after they'd gone in to start the spring-cleaning Honey insisted on, Rose said to Blossom, "Males have it easy. They don't have to wait seven weeks between partners."

"They don't get to carry eggs, though." Blossom wiped a soapy rag along the stairs while Rose scrubbed the kitchen floor. "Have you noticed how obsessed males are with eggs? Much more than females are. Eggs are just a part of life for us, but to males they're sacred."

It was the first time Rose had heard Blossom say something that indicated she had a brain under the sarcasm and gossip. "I hadn't noticed it, but I think you're right."

"I bet Sable's a pounding good fuck, too. All that practice. I'm going to save that newspaper article so I can try every one of those positions with him."

Rose glared. Blossom tipped half the dirty wash water down the stairs, where it pooled in a spot Rose had already cleaned. "Oh, and I need you to take my shop day this week. You owe me."

Honey took spring cleaning seriously. They closed the shop for three days of hard work cleaning, repairing, and painting the co-op building.

As always when it was done, Rose was proud of the results. The place shone and everyone could find things: favorite brushes, sponges, scissors, canvas nails. Rose gessoed over all her old unsold paintings. Only the Foxbury bridge escaped the slaughter. She hung it next to her favorite sky painting as a reminder.

They rearranged the gleaming shop last, rotating in paintings reserved for the new year crowds. Honey had already had a lot of advertising flyers printed, and Sable hung them around town on his way to and from breeding appointments.

To Rose's mingled shock and pleasure, the flyers featured her work this year. "Prominent local artist Rose Blackthorn's last new work before she leaves for a tour of the Southern Lands."

She was really leaving, and she could not possibly return for months—not when Honey had essentially told everyone in White-fall she would be gone.

"Let's see what you've got," Honey said when Rose brought her latest canvases in. "That's a nice stack. Let's go through them now." She flipped through the canvases briskly, giving each a prac-ticed once-over and moving them into piles. "These are the best. We'll put whopping great prices on them and get you some trav-eling money. These are quite good, and these are weaker but still worthy. We'll put sale prices on them. I guarantee they'll all end up on student walls for the spring semester."

After that Rose spent the evening matting her canvases so Honey and Blossom could hang them in the shop. Sable had left mat-ting to the last minute too and they worked side by side at the kitchen table. Rose tried to concentrate on her work instead of being distracted by Sable's musky scent and his nearness. He prob-ably already had someone lined up for the holiday. Hopefully not Blossom.

Rose was tempted to spend the week with Sable, if he would have her. She thought he would. Images of what they could do together kept intruding on her concentration.

"This razor blade is getting dull," Sable said.

"Oh, stop *talking*. I'm losing my mind!" Rose said. After that they worked in sullen silence.

At last the mattes were all in place. Honey affixed discreet squares of cardboard to the backs, with prices and other information printed in her impossibly neat script.

"That's it. Ready for dawn," Honey said after another half hour. The shop looked phenomenal. Rose and the others crowded inside, admiring one another's paintings and making last-second adjustments.

Rose dragged herself upstairs to her room when the group broke up. She was worn out but so nervous about tomorrow's big sale that she was certain she wouldn't be able to sleep.

The night was mild. Rose lay on her newly washed sleeping blanket and listened to an owl hooting from the cedar in the yard.

She shouldn't have snapped at Sable, but perhaps it was for the best.

She still wished Sable would visit her room to return a brush or ask a question. He would be struck by her beauty, overcome—would take her in his wings and whisper his passion.

Rose fell asleep and had interesting dreams.

Four

The new year's sale started at dawn and continued until almost midnight. By the end of the day, everyone was staggering with exhaustion. For once Rose got almost as much attention as Sable, with dragons stopping to ask her questions about her paintings, her plans for the future, and her trip.

She realized quite soon that she had to supply details of the trip or it would sound false—a marketing gimmick. She would be despised. By the time they closed for the night, she had worked out a reasonable itinerary just from talking to potential customers.

The shop walls, so crowded that morning, were much barer now. Rose had sold all the paintings Honey had pronounced as weaker, half the average paintings, and quite a few of the expensive ones. She had been offered a commission, a first for her, but turned it down politely because of her trip. She recommended Sable to make up for snapping at him the previous night.

"We have made out like bandits," Honey said once the shop door was locked behind the last customer. "Cold chicken casserole in the kitchen. Eat up. You'll need your strength tomorrow."

They all laughed as they settled around the table. Tomorrow was the fair, and after that everyone would be busy mating.

Rose thought about the fair while she ate. It was a light-hearted festival in the daytime, with children running about, awful food, ridiculous games, overpriced stalls full of things no one needed but everyone bought, and music. As evening progressed, it became more and more raucous. Those who wanted to choose a mate spent time milling about, flirting in a way that would be outrageous any other time of the year. There was a matchmaking service run by the hatchery to raise funds, and a raffle to bid for particularly attractive mates. By midnight it was guaranteed to devolve into an animalistic spectacle. Inhibitions fell so low that couples would mate in full view, drawing crowds of voyeurs.

"I'm leaving for my trip tomorrow," Rose said. "I'll have the sky to myself."

"Everyone else will be fucking," Blossom said agreeably.

It was another mild night and they all retired to the courtyard after eating. The first fireflies of the year blinked lazily under the cedar, and from the neighbors' yards Rose heard laughter, talk, and distant music. The smell of grilling meat drifted on the breeze.

It was all so impossibly perfect that Rose was struck with nostalgia. She might be like Oriole Sky and never return home, staying instead in a foreign land until its customs seemed normal and the new year's excitement felt like a long-distant dream.

She excused herself and murmured, "I must pack," but instead just stood at an upstairs window and looked down at her colleagues. She would miss them. How dear were their foibles and insecurities, how vast her gratitude for their friendship. She had never told them how much they meant to her.

She retrieved a canvas and paints from her room and set up an easel in the hallway. She didn't intend the painting to turn out good—she might never show it to anyone—but she would keep it to remember this night forever.

In the last few months Rose had worked hard to develop a quick hand, an open style that suggested as much as it showed, but this painting needed a different approach. She smoothed purples and blues onto the canvas as the sky, roughed in the silhouettes of trees and buildings in the distance. The cedar was easy to paint now—she felt it was an old friend. The yard's weedy cobbles were barely visible in the dim light, so she painted a gray-blue background with dark and pale highlights to give the impression of texture. Finally she turned her attention to the figures. She could paint dragons but rarely did, and as a result she doubted her ability to render them as well as the landscapes she preferred.

She painted Sable first, lounging near the cedar with his tail curved in an elegant half-circle. Elm and Blossom lay close together, muzzles nearly touching as they talked. Rose wondered if Sable had turned Blossom down or if Elm had approached her first. Honey and May sat together, May gesturing with one wing as she told a story Rose couldn't hear from the upstairs window.

The figures turned out well, even May with one wing extended and her jaws open as though in laughter or song. Rose paused with her brush over the canvas, about to dab a highlight on May's back. Would that overdo it, look amateurish and awkward? The pose was a difficult one to pull off. Better to stop painting before she ruined it.

She dabbed the highlight on after all. Yes, that looked good. It made May's hide appear to gleam in the starlight, implying a fresh molt.

That reminded Rose to add stars, bare pinpricks scattered across the sky. The brush picked up the background pigment as she painted, so some stars appeared dimmer than others. Lastly she added a few small details to the background shapes, just enough to make them seem better realized.

She was panting when she finished. Oh, skies, it was good. It was *really* good. She added a few greeny-yellow dots beneath the tree as fireflies, then signed her name in the corner.

The painting was far different from her usual work. She hoped she would not wake up in the morning and hate it.

She set the easel in the corner of her room while she cleaned her brushes and put them away. She was mostly packed already: the painting travel kit, her guide book and map, a small blank journal Honey had given her, rolled-up blanket, toiletries kit with tooth-brush, claw file, and oil for her horns—not that she bothered to oil her horns ordinarily, but she might as well make a good impression while traveling. Her water flask was already full and she had some dried meat and oatcakes in a waxed leather pouch for emergencies.

She had put most of her money in savings, carrying enough to make her first few weeks comfortable. She hoped to sell paintings to pay her way most of the time. The rest of the pack was full of blank canvases.

She lay down and closed her eyes. This time tomorrow she'd be far away, hopefully in a clean hostel somewhere. She planned to fly all day and find a reasonably large town in early evening where she could get a good meal. She could reach the Stekkan Mountains within a week if she flew directly there.

She jumped up and wrote a note, tilting the paper to catch more light from the window. The moon had risen. "Honey, you can sell this one for whatever you think fair. Call it 'New Year's Eve.' I love you all. See you in a few months. –Rose"

She wriggled into her pack and settled it along her back between her wings. Then she leaped from the window and winged into the night sky.

Five

Rose's wings cupped the night air as though she had never set foot on land and was instead a creature of sky, like the white swallows that only landed to lay eggs. Every wingstroke carried her away, away, away—into a future she couldn't imagine but could hardly wait to experience.

Within an hour she was flying over patched forest and farmland, all dark under the thin moon. She flew directly toward the nearest border, the little country of Inkle, but she would need to fly for hours to reach it.

For the first time she wondered what on earth she'd been thinking. She couldn't fly all night. It was absurd.

She fretted over the question for some time. Then she encountered a small, warm updraft that lifted her into a tailwind, and the glory of flying absorbed her again.

So be it. She would fly all night and cast herself onto the ground like a vagabond poet in the morning. At least it would make a good story to tell later.

Another hour passed, then another. Rose's eyes kept trying to close. "I should stop," she thought repeatedly. "I should land and sleep." But she didn't.

She dozed on the wing, as she had heard long-flying explorers did while crossing the ocean. That would be terrifying—not sleeping on the wing, which turned out to be quite easy although not very restful—but flying over water with no opportunity to land for days and days.

After another hour, Rose had grown so wretchedly tired that she couldn't make decisions at all. She dithered at the thought of stopping to sleep, or just to relieve herself. Her entire existence seemed tied to this night flight. The moon had set and there were no lights anywhere except the stars. She felt she was the only dragon left alive.

Then, without her understanding why at first, her spirits lifted. Her energy returned.

She noticed a faint paleness to the eastern sky. Dawn was coming! Suddenly jubilant, she cleared her dry throat and crowed the morning prayer as she had not done since childhood. She wasn't religious these days, but the approach of dawn after a long, exhausting night seemed miraculous as it never had before.

The sky lightened as she flew, revealing little clouds in rows. They lit up pink from underneath as sunrise approached. "Fair today, rain tonight," Rose thought.

When the shining rim of sun showed above the horizon, Rose crowed again and sang the morning prayer. As she did, she winged above a huge field of flowers planted in the shape of a flag.

The Inkle flower-flag! She had seen pictures, of course, since it was famous, but she had never seen it in person—and at dawn when she had the sky entirely to herself!

The flag was made of illils, an evergreen plant that bloomed year-round in various colors. She marveled at how many thousands of the plants there must be to make such a large flag, and marveled too at the knowledge that the entire border of Inkle was planted with such flags.

She flew on, growing increasingly hungry. "I'll stop at the first town," she thought, and imagined the lavish breakfast she would order.

There were farmhouses below, singly and in little clusters, but nothing Rose would call a village. She saw a few dragons out and realized she was still flying extremely high—the dragons were scarcely dots far below. She dropped out of the obliging tailwind that had carried her through the night. Some of the farmhouses grew their own small flower-flags, although the pink square in the middle was usually fairly sparse. Perhaps that color was difficult to breed.

Rose thought, "I am now ineligible for the breeding program for at least a year."

It was surprising what a relief that was. In the honest morning light, with no pressure from anyone, she realized her contempt for May's breeding program aspirations stemmed from her own feelings of inadequacy.

She would probably be a good candidate for the breeding program. She was educated, talented, successful, and not bad looking. She even had a stripe of the rare coloration known as royal red down her spine, although it was barely visible against her dark pink hide except just after molting. It might be nice to have match-making done by the breeding program, a guaranteed attractive and skilled mate every few months.

She'd never produced an egg before. She wondered how it would feel to lay one. She'd heard it hurt, and lugging the growing egg around inside you for three months sounded dreadful too.

"I don't want an egg," Rose said out loud to herself, annoyed at her train of thought. "I just want art."

She noticed another homemade flower-flag below, this one larger than most and well-kept. It was close to a handsome farmhouse with a big kitchen garden out back.

The view would make a wonderfully rustic painting, but it needed to be painted from above. It would be difficult.

A stand of tall pines was in just the right place, which seemed like a sign. She swooped down and landed in the top of the biggest tree.

It bore her weight easily in its springy branches. She felt heavy after flying so long and exhaustion swept over her.

"Oh, stop," she said out loud. "You did this to yourself."

She unbuckled her pack and hung it on a branch, then took her painting kit out and wedged it securely in another branch. The sharp smell of pine filled her nostrils, which made her even more hungry than she already was.

She spent a few moments sketching the scene with charcoal, making sure to get the angles of the flower-flag, the farmhouse, and the kitchen garden just right. Then she made up her palette quickly.

It was a different type of landscape than her usual work, more like last night's painting of her friends. She painted the sky first, and although the sunrise was well over she gave the clouds a hint of pink. She dabbed in green to suggest trees in the distance, then roughed in the farmhouse.

It was wood and stone with a shingled roof, varied textures that were fun to paint. She tinted the roof very slightly pink where it caught the morning light. She had a bit of trouble getting the ground right—she couldn't quite mix a shade of green that indicated spring growth—but didn't want to fuss over it too much. It would do. The flower-flag was the most important element anyway.

She wasn't completely happy with the painting when she finished. She wouldn't want it in the shop, but it might be good enough to get her breakfast.

She cleaned her brushes on a rag, packed her kit away except for the new painting, and put her pack back on. Then she coasted down from the tree with the canvas held carefully in her claws.

Before she even landed at the back door, it opened. A leggy female hatchling with lemony hide looked up at her with her wings mantled in surprise.

"Hello!" Rose said brightly, feeling awkward as usual around children. "Are your parents about?"

"Yes," the girl said. She turned her head. "Mum! There's a visitor!"

Mum looked like an older copy of the girl. "Are you lost?"

"No, I'm traveling. I'm an artist." Rose's awkwardness deepened. She must sound demented. "I painted your flower-flag and I thought you might accept it in payment for breakfast?"

She shoved the canvas at the pair. To her relief, both of them went "Ooooh!" in the same admiring tone of voice.

"That's fine! Look how lovely it is!" The mother reached for it.

"The paint's still wet. Don't put your thumb in it or anything," Rose said. "It'll take a week or so to dry."

"It's just lovely. Come along in and have breakfast with us. You can tell us all about your travels. Oh, I'm Goldenrod. This is my daughter, Spring."

"I'm Rose." Rose came into a large, comfortable-looking kitchen with a long table in the middle. "Can I help with anything?"

"No, no. It's just a scratch meal, I'm afraid. We're going along to the fair soon."

"I'm happy with anything. I'm ravenous."

Goldenrod set the painting carefully on a shelf over the sink, first moving a teapot and a vase of yellow illils to make room. It did look good, Rose thought—not her best, but certainly not hack work. She would paint a new version later when she had more time and a more comfortable seat than a tree.

Spring obviously approved of Rose and grew talkative. "You can sit here," she said, pushing Rose toward a particular spot at the table. "That's where guests always sit. This is my place." She sat across from Rose, then jumped to her feet again and retrieved a threadbare cushion from the corner. It boosted her up enough to see over the table properly. "My brothers are still getting ready. They're loopy about the fair. I'm going to win a prize in the duck race. I almost won last year but I got water under my wings and it slowed me down."

Rose had no time to ask what the duck race was because Spring continued almost without breath, "I'm going to eat ever so many petal cakes. Do you have those where you're from? They're *so* good! The pink ones are my favorite but Larch says they all taste the same. I think he's wrong but we're going to try one of every color with our eyes closed and see if we can guess. Larch is my best friend. He lives at the Amberly farm. We're in the same year at school but I'm in the advanced reading and he's only in the regular."

Goldenrod, patting out dough at the counter, said, "Larch is in advanced maths and you're not."

Spring shrugged her wings to show the world how unimportant this was to her. "Well, I'm a better flyer than he is. I'm going to win the duck race."

"What's the duck race?" Rose asked at last.

"Oh, it's *so* fun! It's along the river, at the big bend where it's not so deep, and there are ever so many dragons who enter and last year I came in fourth out of everyone my age. I think I'd better wait to eat petal cakes until after the race. I don't want to feel heavy."

Rose was no wiser about the race but before she could interrupt to ask for more details, she heard the thump of hasty feet on stairs and two nearly grown males burst into the kitchen.

"Hey, hey! A stranger," one said, immediately stopping to strike a pose.

His brother pushed him out of the way. "Get out. I'm starved. Morning, Ma."

"This is Rose," Goldenrod said. "She's an artist. Look at what she painted!"

The boys exclaimed over the painting, although the older one kept giving Rose smoldering looks. It was embarrassing. Rose was glad when Goldenrod said, "Quartz, don't be a pest. Set the table."

The boys' father entered a few moments later, which meant Rose was introduced all over again. The painting was duly admired and, finally, Quartz—who was a mottled gray-brown—brought her a bowl of water. Rose downed it in one grateful gulp, earning a chuckle from him. He refilled it and she made herself only sip even though she was still thirsty.

Goldenrod brought a huge basket of fried dough to the table. "Don't overstuff yourselves. There'll be fair food."

"Yes, petal cakes!" Spring said, grabbing three pieces of dough.

The fried dough was plain but good, slightly sweet and slightly salty, fried to perfection with a crusty outside and tender inside. Rose savored every bite.

Once everyone's first hunger was sated, Goldenrod said, "Where are you from, Rose?"

"Just Dayrill," she admitted. "I was too excited to start my travels and set out last night. I reached Inkle at dawn."

"That's some first-rate flying," Quartz said.

Goldenrod clucked her tongue. "Did you sleep at all?"

"A bit on the wing," Rose said. "I had a good tailwind."

She did her best to answer questions about travel when this time yesterday, she'd breakfasted at home. It struck her as absurd that she should be in this strange kitchen eating fried dough with people whose names she could barely keep straight.

"Are you going to the fair?" Spring asked.

"I hadn't really thought about it," Rose said. "I suppose I might."

"Oh, you ought to!" Spring started talking about the duck race again, but her mother shushed her.

"Come with us, if you like," she said. "It's a bit of a flight but I'm sure you'll think it nothing."

The father, a dragon of few words, gave a rumble as he cleared his throat. "There's an art museum. Free today."

"Oh yes," Goldenrod said. "I've never been but it's supposed to be quite a nice museum."

Rose thanked them, interested in seeing the art and finding a tactful way to separate herself from the family.

Once the meal was done, Rose thought they would set out for the fair. But it took forever to get underway. Everyone had little day packs to carry things in but somehow the children's packs had vanished even though Goldenrod said in an exasperated voice, "I told you to put them by the door. Spring, you had yours on last night. Where did you take it off?"

Spring's pack eventually turned up in an outbuilding where, she said with great surprise, she must have been having a tea-party with her dolls. Goldenrod made her turn out the three dolls, which were homemade from various-colored cloth and showed a great deal of wear. One was missing a wing and looked close to losing the other, while another was leaking stuffing from its belly. It was disturbing, although Rose remembered her own dolls always looked similarly disheveled despite her love for them.

Rose was ready to tell the family goodbye and wing off to some distant land where there were no children when at last the party was ready to go. The younger ones rose into the air with Goldenrod calling to them to "stay within earshot or you'll be sent straight home." The parents flew slowly but Rose felt it was only polite for her to stay with them.

She gathered that a trip into town was a rare treat and assumed it was quite a distance away. To her astonishment, even at the slow pace the adults set, it was only half an hour before a good-sized town came into view along a broad, placid river.

Finally, Rose stood in front of a two-story stone building with "Riverton Art Museum" carved above the door. The family called their goodbyes and Rose waved until they flew off toward the fairgrounds on the other side of the river.

Rose entered the museum, passing brightly colored signs that read "Free Entrance Today!" and "Happy New Year!" She hoped it wouldn't be too crowded.

To her pleasure, there were more guides in attendance than guests. It was a bit sad how excited the guides were to see her. "Happy new year!" they all said as she went from room to room.

The art was a modest, varied collection. Nothing really stood out—there were no famous names among the artists—but it was tastefully displayed. Rose spent a few hours studying it all and was enormously pleased to find one of Honey's pieces given pride of place in the "Modern Masters" hall.

She finished at the gift shop where she bought a pre-stamped postcard, a little metal badge with the museum's logo, and—feeling that she should spend more—a box of assorted candies. She pinned the badge to her pack, dropped a few coins into the donations box, and left the museum.

She heard music and voices in the distance along with the smell of grilling food. It was time to visit the fair.

Six

The duck race, to Rose's delight, turned out to be a race just above the water where entrants had to pick up and set down carved wooden ducks in what amounted to an obstacle course. It was hilarious to watch, with plenty of midair collisions ending in both dragons falling into the water. Rose made sure to watch the under-tens race and cheered when Spring came in second.

Rose also ate one of every color petal cake and agreed with Larch that the flavor was always the same. The cakes were good, though.

There were plenty of tea stalls and Rose slurped down many bowlfuls to help keep herself awake. She kept yawning. She sampled lots of other fair food too, watched several musical performances, and looked at all the stalls but managed not to buy anything.

By then it was afternoon and despite the party atmosphere, she started feeling melancholy—and irritable from the noise and commotion, music and talk. She desperately wanted a nap somewhere quiet. Things would only get worse as the afternoon progressed into evening, too. Already it was getting hard to avoid the heavy-handed flirting from males who didn't interest her, although she made sure to decline with the light-hearted traditional phrases.

She decided it was time to leave Riverton. The map and guide book she carried barely mentioned Inkle so she would need to find out where the next town was. She wanted somewhere too small to have a raucous fair but big enough that she could find a hostel or tavern with a free room.

After a bit of searching she found the Inquiries tent and got in line. It seemed like an unusually long wait, and when she reached the front she realized she'd gotten in the queue to sign up for a race.

"Name?" the attendant asked, pencil poised.

"Rose Blackthorn. Wait—I only wanted Inquiries."

"Next table over. Are you entering or no?"

"What race is it?" Rose asked, feeling stupid with tiredness.

"Adults' two-league." The attendant sounded impatient.

"Oh. All right," Rose said, too embarrassed to back out.

"It starts at four under the big clock." The attendant gave her a cloth number to wear around her neck.

Five minutes later, Rose had a hand-drawn paper map to a nearby town. She wanted to leave immediately but didn't know what to do with the cloth number. She made her way to the big clock—it was unmistakable, an ugly monstrosity of stone blocks with a clock face at the top.

A lot of lean, athletic dragons were milling around already, cloth numbers around their necks. Rose wriggled her way through the crowd, trying not to notice how attractive a lot of the males were, until she found the race attendants.

"Where do I turn my number in?" Rose asked.

"We'll take it after the race, don't worry," the attendant said.

"I don't really—"

"If you'd like to stow your bag behind the desk, we'll keep an eye on it for you."

Rose decided the race was an inevitable part of her day. "Thank you," she said.

As soon as she shucked the bag off, she felt much lighter and cooler. She hung the number around her neck—she was 26—and retreated to the edge of the crowd to stretch her wings.

A few males followed her. "You look like you'll make a good showing," one of them said, mantling his wings to show them off.

The other said, "I haven't seen you in the racing circuit before. Are you from out of town?"

They were both impossibly gorgeous. One had a pale brown hide that seemed to glow with health, the other was green-gray with darker stripes ringing his tail.

Rose thought, "I'm going to act foolish, I know it. I shouldn't have stayed."

Flirting with two at once on new year's was a bit awkward, since males became so single-minded that they literally didn't acknowledge other males, but there were traditional responses to deal with the situation. And flirting on a sunny new year's afternoon was an unexpected pleasure. Rose felt her irritability and weariness melt away.

The head race steward, a granite-colored older female with a no-nonsense air, called everyone together. "Hind paws on a starting block," she shouted. "Number thirty, hind paw on a starting block."

In the scramble, Rose lost track of her two would-be suiters. She placed her right hind foot on the peaked cobble sticking up from the ground. It was made of sandstone and had been worn smooth by other paws over many years.

She glanced around at the other dragons waiting for the race's start. How sleek and lovely they all were! Their eager expressions and alert attitudes made them look similar although they were all different sizes, shapes, and colors.

Would this make a good painting? It wouldn't really work with her style, but she would sketch it later in her travel journal so she could remember the moment.

The red starting flag slashed down while Rose was still admiring the other racers. She was the last to push off from her starting block. She surged into the air amid the glorious slapping of wing leathers all around her.

Once she'd gained height, the cloth number fluttering against her chest, she settled into her usual pace. It only took her half a dozen wing strokes to leave the other stragglers far behind and catch up to the main group.

The river flashed by below. A warm updraft from the park brought the scent of grilling meat to her nostrils.

She saw a tower in the distance with a red flag flying from its flat roof. That must be the midway point, approaching fast. She had never pushed herself, did not know how fast she could really fly.

She pumped her wings, a skimming stride to row herself through the air like a swallow. Her speed increased, the wind a constant roar over her ear membranes. She shot to the front of the crowd with only half a dozen front-flyers ahead of her. By the time she reached the tower, she'd passed two of them.

Two race stewards were perched on the roof between shallow paint trays. Rose pushed herself, dragging air deeply into her lungs and through her bones, but couldn't quite outdistance #17, who was a female the same pink of a rare illil.

Seventeen smacked her right paw in the red paint tray, then used the stone blocks edging the tower to stop herself and immediately push back off for the return flight. It was elegantly done, Rose had to admit.

Half a wingstroke later Rose reached the tower too. The stewards had already whisked a cover over the red paint tray but had removed one from a yellow tray. Rose slapped the paint with her right paw so energetically it splashed, although the tower roof was a riot of colors from hundreds of races.

She backwinged hard, the chalky smell of tempura in her nostrils, and twisted her body so her hind legs met the stone railing. She pushed off again, rolling in midair to right herself—not as elegantly as #17, and requiring another skip of her hind legs on the roof to help find her balance. Then her wings cupped the air again and she soared toward the distant clock tower above dragons still toiling for the paint trays.

Yellow was good. She'd get a ribbon no matter where she finished. But it would be lovely to actually place.

Seventeen had gained two lengths on Rose, her red-paint paw just visible against her side. Rose set herself to beat her.

One stroke, two, three, and Rose edged ahead of #17. The two front-flyers were both males, including the ring-tailed male Rose had spoken to before the race. She did like ring-tails. She would catch up to his, maybe fly close enough that it would dance across her hide as they flew.

Panting, ravenous with a sudden lust deeper than any hunger, Rose closed the gap between them. She barely noticed when she passed the other male.

The park, the river, the ugly clock tower, the cobbled square with a purple paint tray. The ring-tail was #19 and his right paw was purple. He'd been first on the half.

With a grunt of effort, Rose edged him out and hit the purple tray with her left paw an instant before he did.

They collided, tumbling apart in a spattering of paint. Rose had a moment of confusion, then fear for her wings as she bounced off the cobbles. But flying skills bred in a dragon's very bones got her back in the air without conscious effort. She backwinged and skidded to a halt on all four feet.

She blinked in surprise. "Move, move," someone shouted over the roar of spectators. A race steward waved a wing at her urgently at the edge of the square.

It was #19 who tugged her forward, away from the next landing dragons. He hurried ahead of her as they neared the block fence, one wing brushing her back and his tail sliding along her side.

He looked back at her, his eyes dark with passion.

"Do you live nearby?" Rose asked him.

Seven

As soon as the medals were awarded, a double purple for #19 and a single purple for #26, they headed to his apartment. Rose nearly forgot to retrieve her backpack.

He was ushering her into the small but clean bedroom when he said, "Oh, my name's River."

"I'm Rose." It suddenly seemed absurd that they hadn't yet introduced themselves. She laughed, which started him laughing too—the sort of laughter that left them helpless and giggling.

The room smelled of pine cleanser and an intensely male dragon. Rose let herself drop to the freshly scrubbed floor, where she looked up at River. "We're getting paint everywhere."

"I'll get the sponge."

He retrieved a big sponge and a towel from the washroom and stood over Rose a moment, the tip of his tongue just showing and the sponge dripping water down his empurpled arm. He was so adorable that Rose started giggling again.

He sat next to her. "Allow me," he said huskily.

He stroked the paint off her with the sponge, then let her clean him. At one point he murmured with approval, "Royal red," which made her laugh. The stripe of fine red along her spine wasn't as interesting to him as the pale pink of her belly, though. Soon the sponging turned to nuzzling and the sponge and towel lay forgotten.

Rose breathed his musky scent deeply, feeling as though every inch of her skin was hyper-aware of his nearness. His breath as he rubbed his muzzle along her belly sent shocks of desire through her body.

They both froze for a long moment, his mouth just above her vent. She'd kept her vent closed out of habit at first, then effort. No sense rushing things, no matter that she felt all her insides were a glorious fire focused around her vent, and there was only one way to quench the flames.

Slowly, delicately, River slipped the tip of his tongue between the folded edges of skin. Rose gasped.

He lapped her gently, sending pulses of pleasure through her. He lay alongside her, his own vent not far from her head. She moved just far enough to lick the bulge of soft white scales.

River made a sound somewhere between a moan and a whinny. His cock surged out of his vent and up her tongue, hot and hard, and she rubbed it against the ridged roof of her mouth until he cried out and tightened his claws on her hips.

He said in a strangled voice, his words muffled against her belly, "I can't last much longer."

Rose moved her head away so she could speak. "Wriggle around, then. I want you in me."

River stood, his cock waggling ridiculously below him, red and wet, and settled across her hips. She felt the hardness rub along the base of her tail until it reached her gaped vent and slid inside.

Rose wrapped her arms and wings around River and pulled him close. They were both panting. She clenched around him and laughed breathily as he whinnied again. He thrust into her, stoking her fire until she thought she would burn him, and when he released and filled her, she lost herself in the pleasure.

They rested afterwards, exhausted, wrapped in each other's wings. Rose fell asleep but woke to the gentle scrubbing of a freshly wetted sponge along her belly.

"Bright skies," she breathed, astonished at how quickly the fire kindled in her again. "You're as good a lover as you are a flyer."

River chuckled and pressed the sponge against her vent. "Do you realize we're both still wearing our medals?"

It was late when they were both spent. They slept, although Rose woke briefly a few times at the sounds of laughter, voices, and music from the street below.

Overall, Rose thought as she shifted more closely to River in the coolness of the night, she'd had a very good first day of travel.

River had stocked his larder well, which was good since they did little more than eat, sleep, and fuck for the next three days. They only left his apartment once the first day, to walk through the nearby park and listen to birdsong. Somehow they found themselves hidden inside a prickly evergreen bush, coupled together while trying to smother their giggling.

By the end of the third day, their ardor was cooling. Rose spent part of the evening bringing her journal up to date and writing a postcard home before River nuzzled her under the jaw. She set her things aside for another mating session, but it was more perfunctory than passionate. She was tired of feeling sticky and longed to stretch her wings.

"I'd better leave in the morning," she murmured to River.

He stirred. "It's been lovely. I'll take you to breakfast first."

They breakfasted at a nice restaurant full of similarly parting couples. The water bowls were decorated with white flower petals to symbolize eggshell fragments. Rose wondered if she'd lay an egg in three months.

They registered at one of the corner stands and Rose was given a card to turn in at the hatchery with her egg, if she laid one, so the baby's father would be known. Then she and River said polite goodbyes, as though they didn't remember what each other's bodies tasted like.

Rose looked back as she lifted above the buildings in the chilly morning. She could barely make out River's form among the dragons passing up and down the street. Then he was hidden from view by buildings.

Rose flew higher, into the pale blue sky, and angled toward the mountains she knew lay far to the southeast.

Eight

Flying with no particular destination was such a joy that Rose kept moving for the next week. She was over Varrill now, rolling farmland and pastures full of elk and sheep. She only pushed herself the first day, to make up for lost time, and was pleasantly tired when she landed late that evening to find lodging and a meal.

The village was as quiet and old-fashioned as anything she'd imagined when planning her trip. The fading excitement of the new year had scarcely troubled the community, although Rose heard chatter among locals in the tavern's common room about who had "flown off" with whom. It was so quaint she wanted to laugh.

She had a table to herself under a small window. She gobbled elk stew and sopped up the broth with hunks of bread still warm from the oven, then sipped the thin, sour tea that came with it. Its flavor paired well with the food. An older couple came in, shaking rain off their wings, and a half-grown male hurried over to start a fire in the big fireplace.

Rose sighed with contentment and watched raindrops dribble down the windowpanes until she grew sleepy. She considered ordering more tea and joining the group of dragons lounging by the fire, but she hadn't gotten much sleep over the last several days. After her third yawn in a row, she went upstairs to her tiny sleeping room.

It was chilly, but her sleeping blankets were thick and smelled freshly laundered. She took out her travel journal, intending to sketch the low-ceilinged tavern and the locals she'd observed, but as soon as she rolled up in the blankets she was asleep.

The rain blew away overnight, leaving the morning crisp and cold. Rose breakfasted hugely and consulted her guide book. Then, already feeling restless, she took off into the sky.

Over the next several days, she came down frequently for meals and sightseeing. The weather warmed and everywhere she looked there were signs of spring: green trees, newly plowed fields, birds singing, flowers blooming. She could see the mountains now when she flew high enough—still no more than low blue shapes on the horizon, but the land was hillier than before.

After a final scorching day that felt more like summer than spring, clouds gathered and Rose felt the presence of lightning like prickles all over her hide. She had been flying for hours, enjoying the roar of wind over her ear membranes and the hot sun on her back. Now she angled downward and scanned the land ahead for a town.

She saw a few stone towers in the distance and made for them. Thunder rumbled and the wind picked up, tossing the treetops and pushing Rose back and forth. One moment she had to tack hard across a current of wind, the next moment it whirled around to carry her forward far too quickly for safety.

A spit of hard rain fell, then stopped. The towers grew near-er, some old, some newly built, proving that she was nearing a city. She tried to picture the map of Varrill and couldn't remember where she was, precisely. More rain fell as she flew above outlying farms and pastures.

Suddenly the storm was on her, raging in earnest. She only just managed to keep from crash-landing, stumbling on a cobbled street on the outskirts of the city, then ran toward the nearest building through a torrential downpour.

The door was locked, the building dark inside. Rose huddled under the faded green awning for what shelter it provided until, with a metallic scream, the wind pulled it from the building and sent it tumbling down the street.

Drenched and terrified, Rose dived for a narrow alley between two buildings. The wind didn't drag at her so ferociously there. Thunder roared and lightning flashed constantly, but the rain was so heavy she could see nothing.

Wings wrapped tightly around her, she pressed her side against the bricks. They still gave off warmth from the earlier sunshine. The rain eased slightly, then turned to stinging hail.

Rose ducked her head under her wing like a bird and crouched with her belly on the ground. She could hear hailstones rattling off her wing leathers, could feel the temperature dropping rapidly. When the hail turned back to rain she peeked out. The ground all around her was coated with white.

She thought of the stories she'd read of dragons freezing to death, usually when flying too high. How long did it take to freeze? Her toes and tailtip hurt from the cold.

She considered how far she had flown in the last week and a half. If she turned back as soon as the storm abated and flew directly home, it might only take her a few days to arrive.

If anyone asked her why she'd cut her trip short, she could explain that she'd been rained on.

The thunder retreated at last, taking with it the worst of the rain and wind. Rose shuffled through the melting hail until she had space to unfold her wings and shake them. Then she launched into the drizzly air in search of a café.

She was in a bleak, deserted part of the city, full of warehouses, but within a few minutes she was coasting over a much more lively-looking street. Dragons were already out, some of them surveying storm damage, some shopping at a battered-looking street market. A group of small children threw hailstones at each other, laughing.

Rose coasted down and dropped to the puddled street. The neighborhood felt something like home. The buildings were old and not always in good repair, with windows crowded next to each other showing how small the apartments likely were. But many doorways and walls were decorated with murals, the market was doing a brisk business, and dragons called greetings to one another.

Even better, as Rose glanced around, she saw a sign painted in an amateur but artistic hand that read TASSER TEA SHOP & CAFÉ. She crossed the street and entered through the arched doorway, which was propped open.

Inside, the café smelled of high-quality tea and baking bread. It was crowded, though, with every table full. Even the low windowsill overlooking the street had been pressed into service. Two young women were scrunched in the narrow space between the window and two nearby tables, steam from their teapot fogging the diamond-shaped panes.

Rose hesitated, torn between an intense longing for a cup of something warm and not knowing what to do with herself while she drank it.

A lanky gray-green male at a nearby table said, "You look like you got caught in the storm. Scooch over, Juniper. Make room for one more."

"Oh, thank you so much," Rose said. She stepped up to the counter and ordered hastily, then claimed her spot between the male and Juniper, who looked enough like him to be his egg-twin.

"I'm Acorn and this is my sister, Juniper," the male said, "and that's Silver, Meadow, Grove, and Bee. Sorry it's such a cram; Tasser has the best teas but absolutely no space." His words lilted with the local accent.

"I'm Rose," she said, trying to impress all the names into her memory. The young, friendly faces reminded her of her art school days. "I got caught by the storm on the wing."

"That's a scare!" Silver said. She was pale green with darker speckles across her shoulders, the coloration of an eggshell. "Are you all right?"

"Nothing a pot of tea won't fix," Rose said, and everyone laughed.

"You sound like you're from Dayrill. Are you?" Juniper asked.

"Yes, from Whitefall. I'm an artist."

"Oh, so are we!" everyone said.

"We're trying to start a co-op," Acorn said. "Do you have any experience?"

"Yes, actually, I do." Rose was gratified at their excited remarks but added quickly, "I didn't start it myself. It's Honey Bywater's; I've only been a member for about six years."

She immediately felt boastful for dropping Honey's name. "Oh skies, she's one of my favorite artists," Bee said. "She has such an evocative style!"

"She makes me feel like an amateur," Rose confessed, to wry nods. "She's wonderfully helpful, though. This trip was her idea—although I haven't done much painting yet, to be honest."

The server brought her pot of tea, carrying it in both paws and therefore walking clumsily on her hind legs only. Rose was certain she would dump the whole pot over someone's head as she threaded her way between dragon tails, but she set it on the table without spilling a drop.

Rose noted the lack of eatables on the table and ordered enough buns and cakes for everyone. It really seemed scarcely possible that she could rise any higher in the group's estimation.

After an hour, full of good tea and a really awful number of buns, Rose decided that getting caught in the storm was worth it. When Acorn invited her to stay with the group for a few days, she accepted.

They made their way out of the café and down the street in the watery sunset. It was much colder than before and Rose hoped the rolled-up blanket in her pack was dry. She hadn't taken the pack off yet, since there'd been nowhere to set it in the tiny café, and she longed to shuck off the wet leather.

The current home of the future artist's cooperative was a few streets over—very close to where Rose had sheltered from the storm, in fact. "A friend of a friend's cousin owns this warehouse and doesn't mind us living in a corner of it," Silver explained earnestly. Rose wondered if the friend-of-a-friend's-cousin actually knew they were there. They'd fixed the space up nicely, with partitions made of wooden crates stacked sideways to form a wall on one side, shelves on the other. They even had a small common area with a camp stove and mismatched pillows to lounge on.

Rose was obliged to look at everyone's art and critique it, which she did gently. They all had talent but were still so young that only Grove—who was a little older, a quiet male with mottled green hide—showed a well-developed style. Rose found something to praise in every piece, encouraging Bee to work on her figures, Silver her landscapes, Juniper her colorful abstract pieces. As she talked,

Rose thought, "This must be how Honey feels all the time. She's always evaluating our work and guiding us." It made her feel responsible and mature.

When Meadow asked shyly if they could see Rose's latest paintings, she had to explain that she had nothing with her. "I plan to do a sky painting in the morning if anyone wants to join me," she said. "It's been over a week since I put paint to canvas. I need to get some work done."

"Oh, yes, please!" Silver said. "You can give me pointers, if you don't mind. There's a nice hillside not far from here that's got a lovely view."

Rose regretted her plan of painting at dawn when it became obvious how late everyone meant to stay up. Her own school days were far enough behind her that she'd forgotten the impossible hours students kept. They sat around the common area on pillows and talked about art, cooperatives in general and Honey's in particular, and music. That prompted Acorn to retrieve his harp and Bee her absurdly small guitar. Meadow brewed tea and they all ate cheap vanilla biscuits by the pawful from a huge bag Grove set in the middle of the room, and sang old folksongs.

It was fun but exhausting. By the time the talk wound down and people started slipping off to their rooms, Rose was nearly asleep already. She was glad when the room emptied and she could stretch out among the pillows and close her eyes.

Nine

Rose stayed with the young artists for a week. They fed her as much tea as she could slurp down, peppered her with questions, and shared their every enthusiasm with her as though she was a trusted older sister. It was endearing, and Rose reciprocated with advice and shared meals out, which she could afford and they could not. They attended two parties and threw one of their own, painted at all hours of the day and night, and talked talked *talked*.

They asked her to stay a little longer, but Rose refused politely. "It's been a lovely visit," she said honestly, "but I still have so many places I want to travel. I'll write, though, and of course you must visit me once I'm home."

She wrote them each a letter of introduction to Honey. They accepted the letters with respect and awe, which made Rose feel that she'd made the right decision. She hoped Honey didn't mind if they all descended on her at once.

She also left them a painting she'd made of the tea shop they all loved, a view from the street with puddles suggested by quick slashes of color. Rose remembered Honey's rain panting that fateful day months ago, and wondered at how quickly her own abilities had grown.

Then she flew away with relief, because if she didn't get a full night's sleep soon she would drop dead.

She flew hard and fast that day to make sure she hadn't lost fitness after a week eating mostly vanilla biscuits. She didn't stop until it was almost dark, then found a room in a countryside tavern and slept for ten hours.

She woke refreshed, had a sensible breakfast at an outdoor table, and consulted her map. To her surprise, she'd crossed the border to North Stekka without realizing it. She was genuinely far from home at last.

Her cash was running short. It would be nice to sell a few paintings to finance her journey, as she'd planned, but it was no use trying to sell anything in the countryside. She'd need to make her way to a city.

She pushed her empty plate aside and spread the map out all the way. It was a sunny morning and the map was detailed, so Rose lost herself for a time in planning. She'd come from the city of Elkton in Varrill, which was still the closest. The next nearest city was Tirras, which her guide book said was picturesque but modern, tucked in the shadow of the mountains. It was surrounded by farmland and the book assured her that locals were friendly and welcoming. "Make sure to spend a few nights outside of the bustling city and experience life at a more traditional pace," it said.

The tavern keeper emerged from the low building behind her. "More tea, miss?" he asked, blinking in the bright sunshine. He was a very old dragon, bony and faded, but his eyes were clear and he was obviously interested in her map.

"No, I think I'll be leaving soon. Have you ever visited Tirras?"

"Once, a long time ago. That was before your mother hatched, I'm sure."

"What was it like?"

"Oh, it was marvelous." The man sat down across from her. "I went for the new year. More mates to choose from."

She laughed. "Did you fly from here?"

"Yes, and it's the only time I left for more than a day. I found a new year's mate, all right, and at the end of the holiday we decided we were suited. She came back with me. We had six kids, and they've got kids of their own now. It's been a good life, although I've outlived my Feather and the oldest of our children."

"I'm sorry," Rose said gently.

"Well, there's rough with the smooth. They say we all go back to the egg in the end and get hatched anew, so maybe Feather and I will meet again in our next life."

He gathered her dishes up with a clatter and returned inside. Rose sat with the sun warming her back and spring birdsong all around her, and thought about life and death, joy and grief.

She packed her map and guide book away, went inside long enough to settle her bill, and took to the sky. She felt young and full of energy. "I should savor my health every moment of every day," she thought, and tried to pay attention to the strength of her wings, the movement of air through her body. But within five minutes she was thinking of Tirras and whether she would be able to sell some paintings.

Over the next several hours, the land became hillier and wilder, with more forests and fewer towns. Rose landed at a tiny village in early afternoon and was fortunate enough to arrive while the village market was in full swing. She was able to get a good, if plain, lunch of roast chicken, brown bread, and a bowl of vegetables stewed so long they were nearly unrecognizable. She ate everything and mopped the bowl clean with her last bite of bread, consulted her map again, and decided to push on to reach Tirras before nightfall.

The mountains were much closer now, green and brown instead of blue in the distance. As she flew, the hills grew bigger and steeper, a rumpled, unbroken carpet of green as far as she could see. There were no clearings anywhere to indicate a farm or home. The air was more turbulent, but she sailed effortlessly with updrafts that smelled sharply of pine.

The updrafts attracted eagles and other birds she had never seen before. One black and white vulture had a wingspan nearly as broad as Rose's. For a moment they looked at each other, and then the vulture adjusted its feathered wings minutely and soared away.

As the hours passed with no signs of civilization, Rose thought more and more of the vulture. She could die out here and no one but a hungry vulture would know. The guide book said Tirras was easy to find, a large, busy city at the base of three tall peaks. Perhaps Rose had flown right past it. She was within the mountains now but they were huge and there were always more ahead and on either side.

She rode another thermal up and up, spiraling lazily to conserve her strength, until the air was cold and the mountains were mere shapes of green shadows and light far below, an image she was eager to paint. But as she was still rising, she realized with dismay that the mountains weren't mountains. They were only foothills.

The real mountains were still on the horizon, razor peaks topped with white. The sight both thrilled and frightened her. But she remembered the tavern keeper she'd spoken to that morning, who had flown to Tirras in one day. If he could do it, so could she.

Of course, he had probably set off at dawn and had not stopped for lunch and a browse through the local market. But at least she knew now where she was going. Barely visible in the distance were three peaks right next to each other, as sharp as lizard teeth.

Far as they were, she could reach them by dusk. She had a medal in the bottom of her pack that proved she was fast. She might arrive tired out, but she had enough money left that she could afford a good hotel, and of course she could visit the local bank for more cash if necessary.

She turned in the direction of the three peaks and winged toward them.

She had not planned on the thin air at her height. She had enough oxygen to coast like a vulture, flapping her wings only when absolutely necessary, but not enough to move any faster.

It was too cold at this height anyway. Rose angled downward, keeping a worried eye on the three peaks, and took care to stay well above the foothills.

After an hour, the mountaintops still appeared white, which mystified her. She had assumed it was an optical illusion earlier, or clouds. Perhaps the peaks were so steep that no soil could stick to the white stones. Someone in Tirras would know.

The ground below folded into higher hills, deeper valleys. The tree cover was unbroken save for the glint of streams. This wasn't farming country, but the friendly pastoralists her guide book described had to be *somewhere*.

The sunny afternoon faded into evening long before Rose was anywhere close to the mountains. Clouds moved in and obscured the moon.

Rose pumped her wings harder and skimmed forward, scanning the ground below for a spark of light that would indicate a farmhouse. The hills remained dark. Soon the sky was dark too.

She strained her eyes for lights in the distance. But Tirras was still too far away, and the massive foothills shouldering higher and higher all around blocked her from seeing very far.

"I'll just keep flying," she thought. "I flew all night before. I can do it again."

The wind picked up, gusting sometimes frightfully strong. It smelled of rain. Worse, while there were still updrafts to ride, the prevailing wind was against her.

Every draconic instinct she possessed told her she was safest on the wing, especially in a strange land with no other dragons around. But she would wear out her strength by fighting the wind, and the night was already chilly. She needed to find shelter before the rain started.

Her thoughts full of vultures, she coasted lower and lower. She saw the tops of trees below, almost all of them pines and firs.

There was nowhere to land, not enough light to choose one spot over another anyway. She settled in a treetop.

Once she stopped flying, the real force of the wind was evident. The treetop swayed. She climbed down carefully, feeling for each branch in the dark. When there were no more branches below her, she jumped cautiously, her wings half-open to slow her fall. Even so, they brushed against nearby trunks.

She landed on a thick carpet of pine needles. All around her trees creaked and squeaked in protest, but the air beneath the branches was still and as a result, felt much warmer.

Rose wished she had brought one of the waxed canvas tents on display in the excursion shop. Shelter was urgent. The trees would only protect her from light rain, and then only for a short while.

She unbuckled her pack and shrugged it off, then fumbled around in the pocket where she'd stowed her matches. Her paw closed on the little box and the candle too.

A moment later the candle was lit. The relief of having even a tiny light was enormous.

She was on a gentle slope, which in retrospect was a mercy. She might have landed somewhere dangerous without knowing. The scaly trunks of fir trees were all around, with tough-looking ferns growing through their shed needles. Here and there a small rock poked up from the ground too. But there was nothing that could protect her from rain.

She put her pack back on and walked awkwardly, holding the candle in one paw. Its brave flame trembled with the movement.

She was hoping for an outcropping of larger rocks, perhaps even a cave—uninhabited and just big enough for a single dragon. Instead, she found a fir that had toppled against another tree, which was still alive but bent almost to the ground with its dead neighbor on top of it.

It would have to do. Rose held the candle out and peered under the branches. Surely some animal was already sheltering there. But she saw nothing underneath.

She took her pack off again, shoved it ahead of her, and crawled under the branches. They formed a natural tent, hopefully thick enough to keep off the worst of the rain.

She pulled her journal from another pocket in her pack, dripped wax on its cover, and stuck the candle in the wax. Then, both paws free, she took her drying canvases out of the pack, kept separate from each other by two wooden blocks with slotted edges, and set them aside carefully. She took her blanket out next.

After that she rooted in the pack for her emergency food stores. She'd eaten the oat cakes ages ago but the dried meat was still there. She found a half-eaten packet of crumbling vanilla biscuits, a rock-hard bun that smelled all right, and the tin of candies she'd bought at the art museum on new year's. It felt like months ago, not weeks.

It was a poor supper but better than nothing. She'd filled her waterskin before leaving Elkton, fortunately. She put the canvases back in her pack and buckled its top closed, spread her blanket out, and lay down to eat.

She was so hungry that even the bun was welcome, once it yielded to her teeth. She ate precisely half of everything, leaving the other half for breakfast. The candies, which she had assumed would be dreadful, turned out to be fruit-flavored chews and quite good.

By the time she finished, the rain had begun. She heard it first as a faint hissing in the treetops, which increased rapidly. Rose pulled the candle loose from her journal, and was pleased when all the wax popped off the leather neatly, leaving barely a mark. She propped the candle in the needle carpet and opened her journal long enough to write a quick entry.

She finished, "Travel seems to mean being awfully tired all the time, and then you get rained on."

She tucked the journal away in her pack. Then she blew out the candle.

Darkness rushed in. Even after several minutes, her eyes only adjusted enough to mark a difference between the utter darkness beneath her tree tent and the slightly lighter darkness beyond.

She rolled up in her blanket and prepared for a miserable night.

She was still hungry, and she wanted to brush her teeth, but the cushion of pine needles was more comfortable than a mattress or nest of blankets. The wind had died and the trees no longer groaned or creaked. Rose's blanket was thick and although the rain found its way through the boughs eventually, she was surprisingly cozy.

The rain sleeted down, a constant, steady noise. Before she knew it, Rose was asleep.

Ten

When Rose woke, she felt surprisingly rested. Her blanket was damp, but she herself was warm and comfortable.

She peeked out from under the blanket. It was barely dawn and bitterly cold.

She dozed for a while. Eventually hunger got the better of sleep, but rather than brave the cold just yet she snaked one paw out to retrieve her meager rations, and ate and drank while still wrapped in her blanket.

That gave her strength to face the day. She threw off her blanket all at once and crawled out from under her tree tent.

The forest dripped gently. Nothing stirred. Rose squatted to eliminate, kicked pine needles over the mess, and stretched thoroughly. "I'm the first dragon ever to set foot on this hillside," she thought.

She had made it through a night in the wild. Hopefully she would never need to do so again, but she would definitely make sure she had more provisions in the future.

She stowed her blanket, put her pack on, and found room between the trees to launch herself into the air. She had to punch her way through branches, which showered rain and dead needles all over her. Then she was in the open, the gray sky threatening more rain.

She flew slowly, allowing her muscles to warm, and gained height slowly too. She thought, "If I see a farm two leagues from here I'll be so angry." But the trees were unbroken as far as she could see.

The three peaks were still visible in the distance when she gained enough height. "I'll be there by lunchtime," Rose thought. Her stomach growled.

It was an hour or more before she saw the first break in the trees. At first she thought it was a natural clearing, but as she flew over it she was delighted to see grazing animals of some kind, although she didn't spot a house or barn anywhere. There were more clearings with grazing animals soon after, then the first roofs.

Within another half hour she was flying over a vast, broad valley with a river curving through it. It was so large that she couldn't gauge the distance properly. She kept thinking she'd cross it in fifteen minutes or so, but she kept flying and kept flying, and still there was more valley.

She saw clusters of homes and barns, pastures, and newly plowed or fallow fields like patchwork pieces, all different shades of green and brown. Big ponds lined the river, separated by green walkways. She even saw dragons, mere specks from her height, working the fields or traveling the narrow roads with animal-drawn carts.

Gradually the mountain slopes beyond the valley grew closer, until she saw the gleam of light on rain-washed roofs. She'd reached Tirras.

The three peaks were far above her now. It was impossible just how enormous they were, how majestic. Their white tops were so tall they pierced the clouds.

At long last, Rose flew over the edges of Tirras. The city spread up and out across the mountain's lower slopes, the air busy with dragons. She flew up and up, marveling at how large Tirras was. The guide book was correct that it was impossible to miss.

The city didn't seem to have a defined center and she didn't know where to land. Then she noticed a broad, level area with buildings in rows. They looked like businesses instead of homes, so Rose flew closer to get a better look.

Almost the first thing she saw was a building built of pale pink stone. The second was a plaza paved with similar-colored flag-stones, with tidy market stalls at one end and a series of paved yards separated by walls at the other. Each yard contained tables, and many of the tables had dragons eating at them.

She nearly crowed with excitement. She'd found restaurants! And the big stone building, she saw, was a bank.

It seemed like fate. She stopped at the bank, hoping she didn't look as disheveled as she felt, and withdrew enough money to get her through several days, depending on how expensive Tirras proved to be and how lavishly she felt like spending.

While the clerk was stamping her updated letter of credit, she asked, "Where's the best place to eat nearby?"

The clerk was as pale a pink as the building, with light amber eyes that made him look washed-out. He said in a hushed voice, as befitted a bank clerk, "I quite like Harney's just across the square. In fact, I was planning to lunch there today if you'd like to join me. My lunch break is only a few minutes away."

Rose was surprised, but she wanted someone to talk to and even a dull lunch companion was better than none. "I'd be delighted," she said.

They arranged to meet and Rose left to claim a table before they filled up, a suggestion from the banker, whose name was Diamond.

The table duly claimed, Rose sipped a delicate tea from an equally delicate porcelain bowl while she waited. She looked over the menu and was glad she'd visited the bank first. The prices were shocking.

Money was for spending, though, and the tea was very good.

"I think we're going to get some sun soon," Diamond said, settling across from her at the table.

"I hope so. I got rained on last night."

Diamond nodded to the server who brought him a bowl of tea. "You're traveling, I take it?" he asked Rose.

"Yes, and I didn't realize there wasn't a single farmhouse in the hills, much less a village. I got caught in the dark and had to spend the night under a tree."

Diamond's pale eyes widened. "You weren't frightened?"

"Only of being uncomfortable, and it wasn't bad after all—but I'm frightfully hungry."

"I'm glad you're safe. There are terrible things in the wilds, mostly in the mountains but I've heard people say they've seen ghost hounds even in the foothills."

"What's a ghost hound?" Rose asked.

Diamond gave his head an agitated little shake. "A horrific beast. It's not nice to talk about at lunch. You're from Dayrill?"

They talked about Rose's travels until the server returned. Rose was determined to eat something she had never tried before and ordered the wild mountain goat casserole, one of the most expensive items on the menu.

After the server left again, Diamond said, "I should travel more. I like to visit the seaside but that's really the only place I go. What are your plans for Tirras? Are you staying long?"

"I think so. I want to try selling some paintings and I definitely want to explore."

"There's lots to do in Tirras." Diamond tilted his head slightly, regarding her from half-lidded eyes as though evaluating her. She had seen the same expression from art dealers who visited the shop at home. "If you're not too tired this evening I'm joining some friends to see a new play. We have a box so you won't need a ticket, and we'll probably find somewhere to eat afterwards. We'd love to have you along."

"That sounds like fun, thank you." Rose wondered what kind of play appealed to bankers.

Their order came and Rose picked up her fork with a trembling paw. Diamond said something but she was so focused on her food that she didn't hear what. The smell alone made her mouth water.

It was just as good as she'd dreamed the previous night, save that she had never had this dish before. It was rich with gravy and shreds of tender meat, vegetables, and a mild and toothsome grain she didn't recognize.

She didn't stop for breath until she'd eaten half her bowlful and taken the edge off her hunger. She glanced at Diamond and said, "Sorry, I'm not a very good lunch companion today."

After that she did her best to be entertaining. Diamond wanted to know about her week spent in Elkton, so she exaggerated the absurdity of her stay with the young artists to make him laugh. He made her laugh too with his quick-witted comments, until she decided the evening would most likely be fun and she should stop assuming bankers were boring.

Diamond wore a long silver chain around his neck with a pendant hanging from it. Rose thought it was mere decoration, and noticed similar chains on other dragons dining nearby, until he sat back, pressed a hidden latch on the pendant, and opened its front to reveal a tiny clock. "I should start back soon. Shall we meet outside the bank around seven tonight?"

"I'll be there, thanks."

They settled their bills, which left Rose almost as poor as she'd been before her bank visit. Once Diamond left, she put her pack back on and went in search of a lodging house.

She coasted over the city, flying slowly to look at the streets below. She noticed squares of pink painted on roofs, which gave way suddenly to squares of blue. Her guide book had a map of the city divided into colors, which she realized were reflected in the roof patches. It was an ingenious system to make it easier for people to orient themselves in the air, and Rose was delighted she'd figured it out on her own.

She landed again in the blue section and hurried along a narrow street paved with stone cobbles, looking for a place where she could stop to examine the map. Unlike the pink stone pavers near the bank, these were gray-blue. She also noticed that many buildings were painted blue or had blue awnings or signs. There were a lot of other dragons hurrying up and down the street: young mothers with hatchlings in tow and shopping bags slung over their backs, workers on their lunch breaks walking briskly, even a small group of older schoolchildren dawdling near a café before they returned to their classes. The students were in everyone's way, squawking with laughter.

The café had a few empty tables outside on a rear veranda. Rose decided she could do with more tea and something sweet, and ducked under the leather flap across its doorway.

She took her time over her tea, sticky bun, and guide book, making plans. If she was going to stay in Tirras a good long time, she needed to find a lodging house where she could both paint and keep her new pieces until they dried. It would be nice to work on bigger canvases too, ones larger than her pack could hold. And she needed to find where to buy paints and canvases and all the other tools of her trade.

She'd pictured herself painting along a quaint river, couples strolling through a park behind her and occasionally stopping to buy a piece. Now that she needed to sell some paintings, she realized how absurd her dreams had been. Hoping for sales from passersby was for students and amateurs.

In other words, she needed a gallery.

Her guide book assured her that the green section of Tirras was the most affordable. It read, "The cafés and gathering places in Green are an exciting mixture of students, apprentices, and entrepreneurs, but it is also a place of poverty and potential danger. You may encounter beggars or burglars. The traveler on a budget will find this section of Tirras a relief compared to prices elsewhere, but should be careful not to leave parcels unattended. Beware also the swindler or cheat who proposes games of chance that seem a 'sure bet.'"

Rose hoped Diamond would not prove to be a swindler or cheat. Still, she knew where he worked and could complain to his supervisor if necessary.

She thought of the drab, reserved Diamond and almost laughed.

She swallowed the last of her tea, feeling rather awash, and put her guide book away. Green was further down the mountain to the east. She would go there first to find a lodging house.

It was early afternoon, still overcast and breezy. The clouds were starting to tear into pieces as they approached the three mountains above Tirras, giving glimpses of blue sky, but the air still felt heavy with potential rain.

Rose flew slowly, since she wasn't sure where she was going and there was quite a lot of air traffic. She had never seen so many dragons in one place and she knew precisely one person among them to talk to. The thought made her feel very small and lonely.

She thought of the artists she'd stayed with in Elkton. She missed their friendliness and earnest pursuit of art. She wished for the first time that she was their age, just embarking on her own journey.

"You ninny," she said out loud to herself, which made a passing dragon glare at her. "You're *literally* on your own journey right now."

The buildings were smaller as she approached Green, closer together and often in poor repair. Many of the green patches painted on roofs were flaking or faded. The land was steeper here as well, without as many flat spaces for the parks, promenades, and terraces in more prosperous parts of the city. But as Rose coasted down to fly just above narrow, crooked streets lined with crumbling houses, she saw how picturesque the views were.

Diamond's bank would make a staid painting destined for some businessman's office. In the right light, these crumbling homes would become *art*.

She flew low enough to look at signs as she passed, hoping to spot a lodging house. There were, it turned out, a great many lodging houses in Green. They were all shabby and they were all full.

After her third "No Vacancy" sign, she started counting. At sixteen she gave up, landed next to a newsagent's kiosk, and asked the newsagent for advice.

He was a middle-aged dragon, paunchy around the middle with a mottled gray and pink hide. "Buy a paper," he said. "Want ads in the back."

She bought a paper and stood in front of his kiosk to read it, just to spite him. The kiosk was next to a corner greengrocer's shop that smelled of rotting fruit.

"I'm soft," she thought. "I've spent too much time in fancy restaurants, not enough time with starving artists." But everyone in Elkton had been friendly, even when they hadn't a coin to spare.

There were more "room needed" adverts than "room for let" adverts. The weekly prices were still high compared to home, too.

Finally Rose scanned down the list until she found the most expensive room she could afford without withdrawing more money from the bank, then annoyed the newsagent further by getting her guide book out and consulting the map of Tirras. Only when she was certain she knew how to find the lodging house did she leave, not that anyone else had come up to buy a paper while she had the newspaper spread out on the narrow dirt road.

She had almost resigned herself to another bank visit and a lodging house in a more expensive part of town, but to her surprise, not only did she find the lodging house easily, it proved to be nicer than the ones she'd seen before *and* still had a room free. A woman with hide a lovely shade of yellowy-green, although it was faded with age, led her up a flight of creaking stairs to a much larger room than Rose expected.

The room had a mattress with a folded blanket on top, a table under the single window, and a smaller table with a lamp on it. "It's not much," the woman said, puffing slightly from the climb. "I keep it clean here. I'll thank you not to bring any males home with you."

"I still have five weeks left in my egg months anyway," Rose said.

"I don't do meals but the café across the street isn't bad. Most of my residents eat there. There's a water pump in the side yard, latrine out back."

"I think it will do, thank you," Rose said. "I'm an artist—I'll be painting. Will the smell of turpentine bother anyone?"

"Not if you make sure to open the window. Don't get paint on my floor."

"Of course not," Rose said, with guilty memories of all the times she'd dropped paint tubes or brushes at home.

She paid her first week's rent and received her key solemnly. The woman left her to get settled in, and Rose took her blanket out and hung it over the table to dry. It already smelled musty. She hoped the weather improved soon so she could open the window.

Next she poked around the room. The table under the window had a deep drawer underneath that held a water jug and basin, which made her realize how much she wanted to wash and brush her teeth.

She took the jug downstairs and outside to find the water pump. Carrying it back up the stairs was more difficult. Rose had never been good at walking on her hind legs only and the trip required a great deal of wing flapping for balance. But having wash water in her room suddenly felt like the pinnacle of luxury.

She brushed her teeth and washed her paws in the basin, but had to dry them on her already damp blanket. She would have to buy a towel.

That reminded her that she needed to get more money from the bank before it closed. Not the big main bank where Diamond worked, though—she was too embarrassed to return there so soon after her first withdrawal. She consulted her guide book again, found a smaller bank in the prosperous Blue district, and was about to leave when she remembered her paintings.

She took them out and evaluated them as honestly as she could. The two best were already dry, fortunately. One was the dawn sky above Elkton, the rooftops still in shadow with hints of reflected light, the sky brighter: a depiction of that breathless moment before the sun edged above the horizon. The other was the street market in Elkton as she had first seen it, everything bright and puddled, shoppers investigating dripping produce at the nearest stall. She was proud of that one and had considered sending it home for the shop.

The others were sky studies, quite nice ones but less inspired. She was growing tired of sky studies, in fact. She had grown so efficient at capturing the sky's changing moods that it was no longer a challenge most of the time.

She gathered up her necessary belongings and left. It was a relief not to drag her pack around, but she worried she would drop something. She added "shopping bag" to her mental list.

Eleven

Rose half-expected Diamond to be in this bank too, but the clerk was a female with hide almost the same shade of pink as Rose's. When she turned to retrieve something from the filing cabinet behind her, Rose checked to make sure the clerk didn't also have the same stripe of royal red down her spine. She did not, which was an odd relief.

Rose withdrew enough money this time to see her through a week. She needed to buy painting supplies. The amount made a big dent in her savings, which made her even more determined to find a gallery to sell her work.

First, though, she needed a bag. She would drop her money in the street without one. It was galling to think that she had the perfect bag at home, roomy cloth with a long cross-body handle, striped in blue and yellow. But she had not thought to bring it.

She found a cluster of shops nearby and almost immediately found a bag she loved. It was made of soft leather with an elegant design printed in black ink on the front. It wasn't as big as her bag at home but it had the same long handle.

The shop was quite a nice one. Rose checked the price, tried the bag on, checked the price again. She should put the bag back and find one that was less expensive. But she really, truly *loved* this bag. It would last her for years if she took care of it! She ought to buy it as a souvenir.

An elegant young clerk noticed Rose dithering and said, "That bag comes with a free keychain."

Rose, trying to juggle her paintings, her paper pouch of money from the bank, her bank documents, her guide book, and her room key, said, "I'll take it."

The paintings fit in the bag. Suddenly unencumbered, even if her money pouch was much lighter, Rose walked through the streets of Blue with the bag nestled snugly between her left front leg and her side just in front of her wing.

The ideal art gallery would be small, she decided, with a variety of painting styles from different artists. It was no use looking in the pink section of town, the most prosperous area, since those galleries would only represent the most famous artists. But there was no point in wasting her time on a gallery that couldn't sell her paintings for what they were worth.

She saw a building painted pale blue, with round windows and a perfectly round wooden door, instead of the more usual square or half-circle. A sign above the door read, "The Sunny Garden Gallery."

Rose hesitated. The place was bigger than she'd imagined. But perhaps that was good after all—they would have more space.

It couldn't hurt to *look*, anyway. She needn't say anything, if the level of skill seemed too high for her modest paintings. She could pretend to browse, then leave.

Her stomach churning with fear, Rose opened the round door and went inside.

It smelled faintly of paint inside, such a familiar scent that Rose relaxed a fraction. The interior was one big room with a counter near the door. A pale pink dragon with faint yellow dapples on her back greeted her pleasantly, glanced her over with a practiced eye, and said, "I'm not taking on new clients but I'm happy to look at your work."

"What? I—I—" Rose could not understand how the women knew she was an artist.

"Your paintings. The corners are distinctive in a bag like yours."

"Oh." Rose slumped, embarrassed at her stammering. She shuffled back a step. "Sorry to bother you. It's a lovely gallery. I mean, I'm sure it is."

"Are you from Dayrill?"

Rose felt light-headed suddenly. Surely this pretty young woman could read her mind—could read everything about her as though her whole life was a guide book titled *Rose Blackthorn.* "Yes."

"Your accent," the woman said. Even her understanding tone seemed designed precisely for Rose's ears.

Rose took a deep breath. Honey would be rolling her eyes if she knew Rose's discomfiture. Blossom would be *howling.*

She stood up instead of crouching in deference, drew the paintings from her bag, and said in as businesslike a voice as possible, "I'm taking a traveling sabbatical from Riverside Art, Honey Bywater's co-op in Whitefall. Maybe you know a gallery that could carry a few of my paintings? I'll be staying in Tirras for a month or so."

She wasn't sure if Honey's name carried any weight this far from home. The woman sat up and took the paintings, set them on the counter, and looked them over for several minutes.

Rose did not fidget. She did not say a word. She did not try to guess what was going through the dragon's mind or what she would say. Instead, she glanced around the room at the paintings hanging on the walls and displayed on easels.

The work was quite good. Some of it was very good indeed. But, she thought, it was no better than anything they could display in the shop at home. She felt a surge of affection for her colleagues and their great talent.

The woman said, "Are these your only pieces right now?"

"The only ones that are dry," Rose said with a flicker of hope. "I'm hoping to do some larger pieces soon."

"I think I can fit you in after all."

The woman's name was Dawn and she owned the gallery. She offered to matte the paintings for Rose, gave her the addresses of artist supply shops that weren't too expensive, and drew up a quick contract once they agreed to terms.

Rose, in turn, helped Dawn rearrange a corner of the shop to make room for her pieces. They were still at it when some customers came in, an elderly green dragon and a young man with a darker green hide but an overall similar look, save that she was confident and he drooped sullenly.

Rose pretended to be busy while Dawn dealt with the pair. The woman glowed with health—or, Rose thought cynically, a top-notch beauty regimen. No one could have that sort of youthful hide at her age without expensive buffing and moisturizers, not even right after molt. When she spoke, her voice was strident and carrying.

Rose thought, "A woman used to being obeyed. I bet that's her grown son—or even grandson. I bet she orders him around and he has to grovel so she won't cut him out of her will."

She adjusted a painting minutely and was amused when the older dragon ordered the man to hold her purse and he replied, "Of course, Grandmother."

The woman demanded that Dawn show her all the latest paintings, which was tiresome. Rose had already run out of things to pretend to do. Dawn took seven or eight paintings down and spread them out along the counter.

"Rose, could you be a dear and matte these new pieces? You can use the materials upstairs." Dawn nodded at a staircase in the corner, half-hidden by a wooden partition.

"Certainly," Rose said, pretending to be an assistant. It was kind of Dawn to give her a reason to leave the room.

The old woman said sharply, "Let me see. You said they're new?"

"Yes, madam," Dawn said. "They're by a marvelous young artist from Dayrill, Rose Blackthorn. We just received them. They won't be on display for another day or two."

Rose thought that surely the woman would make the connection. She imagined saying, "Yes, it is *I*, the great Rose Blackthorn from Dayrill, at your service." Maybe she should bow.

But Rose was a common name. The woman only said, "I like this one. How much is it?"

Dawn and Rose had already agreed on prices for the pieces, although they weren't yet labeled. To Rose's astonishment, Dawn named a sum twice the agreed-upon price.

The old woman said, "I'll take it!" with a note of triumph in her voice.

Rose hovered, stunned and uncertain. Surely she couldn't have sold one of her paintings so quickly. But Dawn was assuring the woman she'd made a good choice, that Rose's work would only appreciate in value as her fame grew. Rose felt as though they were talking about someone else.

"Shall I matte it for you, madam?" Rose asked timidly.

"No, no. I'll take it to be framed."

In the end, the woman bought Rose's street market painting and two other pieces. Her grandson paid and Dawn wrapped them in tissue paper and tucked them into the carryall he wore over his back. The carryall already held a number of other purchases.

When the pair left at last, Dawn closed the door behind them and said quietly, "I wish she wouldn't buy so *many* paintings. No one ever sees them."

Rose was trying to work out her percentage of the sale price and kept coming up with an absurdly high number. "She must have a lot of money."

"Too much." Dawn returned to the counter. "She's built an enormous house on the river beyond the hatchery. It used to be my favorite spot for picnics and now there's a great ugly house there with guards to keep you from flying too close. As far as I can tell she does nothing with her time but shop for things to fill the house, art and furnishings of all sorts—and who gets to see them? No one. Art should be *seen*."

Dawn never raised her voice but Rose felt the intensity of her words as though the dragon was shouting.

Dawn continued, "If that house was mine, I'd open it to the public as a museum. But her family won't do that when she dies. They'll fight over all those belongings for years, then sell them. They don't care what the paintings look like. They only care what they're worth. Anyway, we've only got one piece of yours now. How soon can you bring me more?"

Rose was distracted now at the thought of a giant house full of paintings, locked up tight. "What? Oh, I'll bring the others for you to evaluate this afternoon." That sounded better than "they're not as good."

"We're open until eight but I leave at four. I'll tell my assistant to expect you."

Rose left with her bank pouch bulging again, which was a relief, but with a new sense of anxiety about whether Dawn would accept her other paintings.

She stopped on the way back to her lodging house and bought two towels, a good supply of snack foods, and some postcards. The city clocks rang four while she was flying low over Green, looking for the right rooftop. She hadn't had trouble finding the correct street earlier but it seemed to have vanished.

She recognized it suddenly and swooped down to land, as though if she didn't hurry it would disappear again.

Her room was as she left it. Rose flipped her blanket over so it would dry evenly. Just touching the blanket made her long for a nap—but she had too much to do.

She put the other paintings into her pack and buckled it on with a sigh. It looked like the clouds were clearing off at last, so she opened the window and launched herself from the sill instead of going downstairs. Then she had to turn right around, grumbling with irritation, to lock the door.

The shop assistant had been well prepared by Dawn and took her paintings with a warm, "Oh, these are lovely." Rose left again with relief and went to find the art supply shops next.

They were all in the yellow district, not far from Green. As soon as Rose saw the neighborhood she regretted her haste in finding a Green lodging house. Yellow wasn't that much more expensive and had the youthful, artistic feel she craved. The shops were well kept, if small, and there were handmade posters advertising shows of all sorts, from music to art to theater. She felt that her guide book had misled her.

She first visited the supply shop that Dawn had recommended most highly. As she entered through the propped-open door, she imagined falling in with a group of young artists who might be shopping too. They would surely prove as welcoming as the group in Elkton. But when her eyes adjusted to the shop's dark interior, the only dragon in sight was the shopkeeper. He turned out to be gruff and seemingly bored with his job.

Rose stayed businesslike, but she remembered the old woman paying an inflated price for Rose's painting and made sure she was polite too. When she left the shop, her bag was heavy with all the things she'd bought and she carried a selection of pre-stretched canvases.

She flew home with them and was glad she'd left her window open, although in retrospect she supposed it was lucky no one had stolen all her belongings while she was gone. She was able to fly in through the window and drop the armload of canvases instead of dragging them upstairs.

"I don't have an *easel*," she groaned aloud, and left again to buy one.

By the time she returned and set the inexpensive easel next to the window, it was growing late. If she didn't leave soon, she'd miss Diamond and his friends and wouldn't have anyone to talk to. Friendly people seemed rare in Tirras.

She scrubbed herself clean quickly with the corner of one of her towels, then oiled her horns properly for the first time in ages. She had no mirror so closed the window to examine her reflection in the glass panes.

Then she repacked her new bag with money, room key, guide book, and her journal and a pencil, trotted down the stairs, and flew toward Pink with a sigh of weariness.

Twelve

Rose arrived at the bank just as the bells rang seven o'clock. Diamond gave her an approving nod as she dropped lightly to the paving stones next to him.

He had oiled his horns too and his pale hide gleamed in the weak sunset light, which washed the pink stones with a darker red. In addition to the silver chain around his neck, he wore a bag similar to hers, although it was pink-dyed leather instead of dark brown.

"I'm glad to see you. I thought you might be too tired to come," he said.

"I am tired, but you're almost the only person I know in Tirras. Besides, I want to see the show."

"It should be a fun one—a comedy, I'm told. Robin's the actress in our group; she keeps up with the theatre even when she isn't actually working. We'll meet her and the others at the Precipice. It's not far."

Rose noted that Diamond was looking her over carefully—not like she was a potential mate, but with the same discerning expression she'd seen on him at lunch. She got the impression that she passed some kind of test, since his tone turned warmer as he spoke.

They walked to the Precipice instead of flying. Diamond obviously knew this part of the city well and took her along smaller streets and footpaths that skirted the backs of buildings. It was growing dark quickly and Rose marveled as electric lamps came on all around. She had seen electric lights before, but never so many in one place.

The Precipice was built on the edge of a square, although it was actually more of a crescent shape with corners. Rose had already noticed that flat space was in short supply in Tirras, so flat open areas showed off Pink's prosperity. The theatre building itself backed up to the top of a cliff. A low fence was built along the edge to keep people from stumbling over by accident, although the roofs were far enough below that even a clumsy dragon could get air under their wings in time to soar away safely.

The Precipice was a tall building with a broad covered porch lit with electric bulbs. Dragons stood around talking on the porch and in the square, or walking slowly in an elegant promenade in pairs or groups. Electric lights gleamed off of necklaces and beaded bags, and some dragons even had gold or silver rings on their horns. Rose wondered at the style and tried not to stare at one young woman so beringed that her horns barely showed.

"We usually meet inside," Diamond said. He led the way up the broad steps onto the porch. The porch floor was the same pink stone common throughout the district, but when she and Diamond entered the theatre lobby, its floor was made of pink and green tiles. The walls were a combination of gorgeous mosaics and carved wood screens—sometimes both, with a screen half-hiding a mosaic.

Rose slowed to admire the walls until Diamond said, "There they are. Come meet everyone."

She hurried to catch up as he joined a group of three dragons. They were all young enough to be lovely, old enough to have a full adult's confidence—the same as she and Diamond, Rose supposed. She felt oddly as though she belonged with the group.

"You brought a friend," a woman said, eyeing Rose with interest. She was mostly a soft brown, but with a splash of bright pink on her chest.

Diamond said, "Yes, we met only today. Everyone, this is Rose Blackthorn. She's a painter from Dayrill who will be staying in Tirras for a while."

The three introduced themselves and Rose did her best to impress the names in her memory. The first woman was Robin, the actress, who was friendly but who reminded Rose uncomfortably of Blossom at home—save that Blossom had very little curiosity about others. Rose felt that Robin was drinking in every detail about her, so that she could portray a Rose caricature one day onstage.

Crystal was pale green with darker dapples and wore a single pair of silver horn rings. She was lightly built and looked frail and lovely, but her voice was strong and definite. "I write books," she said.

Rose had never met an author before. "Are you a scholar or a story-maker?"

"Oh, a story-maker. I don't have the patience for research."

Robin said, "We've often talked about it and agree that acting and writing stories are alike in some ways. The important thing is to convey a believable character. Maybe painting is similar."

"Maybe so," Rose said, turning the idea over in her mind. "I paint a lot of landscapes but my goal is to evoke a feeling—or even better, a lot of different feelings."

The third dragon, a gray-green male with striking gold eyes, said, "That sounds like a sort of characterization to me. I'm Elm."

"Pleased to meet you," Rose said. "One of my best friends at home is named Elm."

"Then I hope we shall be friends as well."

Diamond said, "Elm is a lawyer and is running for public office this summer."

"That's exciting. I hope you win."

"Thank you. It's something of a tradition in my family. Both my parents were city councilors and three of my grandparents, so if I don't serve at least one term they'll all think me a failure."

The others laughed so Rose did too. She hoped she could find time to talk art with Robin and Crystal later.

"Here comes Evergreen," Crystal said.

Diamond said to Rose, "It's Evergreen's box. He very kindly lets us use it whenever we like."

Rose turned to greet the new dragon and was surprised when she recognized him. He was the sullen young man who had carried his grandmother's purchases.

He looked much happier now, a strut in his step as he joined the group. He wore a black leather bag decorated with lumpy pieces of gold, gold horn rings, and a gold timepiece around his neck. The gold contrasted nicely with his dark green hide, although Rose thought so much of it seemed ostentatious. But, she reminded herself, she didn't know him. He might have a heart of gold as well.

"Evergreen, meet our new friend," Diamond said.

Evergreen noticed Rose and raised his wings slightly in surprise. "I saw you today," he said. "You're a shop girl at some art place."

His tone was disapproving and Rose was hard-pressed not to fully mantle her own wings. Instead she forced a laugh. "Oh, no, let me tell you what happened. Pleased to meet you properly, by the way. I'm Rose Blackthorn."

She gave her full name on purpose, but Evergreen didn't react. Robin said, "What happened?"

Rose told the story of having to play a shop assistant while her own painting sold at a huge price, and was proud of the way she made it sound genuinely funny. It was funny, she supposed, if you took out all the real emotion of the event.

The others laughed, at least, and that was the important thing. Even Evergreen chuckled and said, "Grandmother got the biggest frame she could find for that thing. I had to drag it around all afternoon."

"Serves you right." Crystal gave him a flirty duck of her head to show she was kidding.

Robin said, "You make such a lovely porter, your grandmother is doing you a favor, really."

"It's only until the old bag drops dead, anyhow," Evergreen said. "She can't last that much longer."

Rose was shocked, but judging from his friends' lack of reaction, Evergreen spoke this way all the time. Perhaps it was only a coarse joke. Elm said, "She'll outlive us all just for spite."

"If she makes me move her hideous statues around again, I'll drop one on her head."

Diamond glanced at Rose and said, "Let's go up and get settled." Rose wondered if her discomfort at the conversation showed.

Evergreen led the way to one of the broad staircases that curved up to a balcony overlooking the room. "Let's order something. I'm starving," Robin said.

Evergreen said over his back, "I already put an order in for tonight. It should be waiting for us."

Rose had been to the theatre plenty of times, mostly with May, who liked outings but only with a companion. As she climbed the shallow steps with the vaulted ceiling far above, Rose thought, "May would love it here!"

A moment later she thought, "May wouldn't like the people I'm with, though." Then she wondered what had prompted the reflection. Evergreen, she supposed, but she was certain May wouldn't like any of her new companions.

Rose wished, with a sudden stab of homesickness, that May was with her.

She had never been in a proper theatre box before. It was open at the front, overlooking the floor far below and the large stage with its curtains closed. There were big pillows to lounge on and a long table loaded with plates of food.

"Good," Evergreen said, surveying the table. "They remembered the punch. I had to speak to someone last time."

Robin grabbed a dainty triangular sandwich in each paw and sat back on her haunches to eat. "I remember that," she said with her mouth full. "You had the poor girl practically groveling on the floor. It was distasteful."

Rose agreed. Evergreen went down even more in her estimation.

He said, "If people would just do their jobs properly, the world would be a better place."

Robin swallowed and said, "You've never done a job in your life. You don't know what it's like to forget a detail and be chewed up about it."

"I don't forget details," Evergreen said. Rose remembered he had forgotten her family name. "Anyway, I work for Grandmother and she chews me up all the time."

"Oh, don't talk about her. It puts you in a sour mood." Crystal ladled punch from a painted glass bowl into a matching paw-sized bowl. "Here, have some hard-won punch. It smells good."

After her huge lunch and all the tea she'd drunk that afternoon, Rose was surprised at how hungry she was when she looked at the food. It was just nibbles, really, nothing substantial, and Robin was shoveling it in so fast that Elm complained. "You'll gobble it all up. What fillings are in the sandwiches?"

"Some of them are spiced ham and the others are spiced lamb. That rhymes. I'm so hungry these days I think I might be growing an egg."

"Or you're just getting plump," Crystal said, glancing at her own trim sides with a self-satisfied air.

"I'll fly it off later this week." Robin shoved another sandwich in her mouth. "I like the lamb best, I think. Rose, come have some of this."

Crystal said, "The punch is lovely. Here, I'll get you a bowlful."

Rose accepted the bowl, feeling awkward. "Thanks. I ate so much earlier I don't know why I have an appetite now."

"Growing an egg?" Robin glanced Rose over. "You don't look round, but of course it's only been a few weeks from new year's. Were you already traveling then? Did you take a mate?"

Rose sipped the punch, which was a blend of juices she didn't recognize. It was both sweet and tart enough to make her jaws ache pleasantly. "I started my travels on new year's eve. I didn't get far, just to Inkle, where I spent three days with a handsome ring-tail."

"Ooh, yummy," Robin said, clearly not talking about the food this time.

"I don't like ring-tails. A nice solid-colored male, that's for me." Crystal gave Evergreen a quick look and Rose wondered if he'd been her mate over new year's or if she was flirting for the future, after her egg months.

Elm asked Robin about the show and she told them all the actors in it and which ones were best. Rose ate little sandwiches and flaky cakes made with honey, sipped her punch, and listened politely. What a difference one day made! This time last night she was looking for shelter in an empty land; tonight she was surrounded by elegant dragons with not a care in the world.

The show proved to be just as good as promised, although a lot of the jokes went over Rose's head. She didn't know the local events and people referenced. One character was named Royal Red, and every time someone addressed him they rolled their Rs impressively. He was obviously based on someone real, and before long everyone in Evergreen's box was howling with helpless laughter and clutching pillows. Rose wished she could appreciate the humor properly, although when the character was doused with yellow paint through a complicated turn of events, and someone addressed him as "Rrrrrroyal Orrrrrange," she laughed as hard as everyone else.

After the show finished, Diamond suggested they get a proper meal somewhere. The hallway behind the curving row of boxes had been transformed into an outside balcony during the show, with panels folded back, so they were able to leave without getting caught in the crowds streaming from the main floor. As they soared above the streets, Rose hoped the chilly evening air would wake her. She was getting awfully sleepy.

Elm chose the restaurant, and Rose wasn't surprised that it was hideously expensive. Still, she had the money, thanks to Evergreen's grandmother.

They discussed the show while they waited for their food. Mostly everyone wanted to talk about the Royal Red character. Diamond said, "I almost invited Flame tonight. Skies, I'm glad I didn't! He'd have exploded."

Everyone laughed. Robin said, "He'd have been too busy courting Rose to notice. She's got royal red right up her spine."

Rose, glassy-eyed with exhaustion, was startled at being the center of attention suddenly. "I don't understand," she said, too tired to attempt wittiness.

"Oh, Flame is a friend of ours," Robin said.

"A prince," Crystal said, a touch of sarcasm in her voice.

Diamond sipped his tea. "He's definitely a prince. He's explained it to me in painful detail."

Robin sat up and imitated one of the actresses in the play. "It's rrrroyal rrrrred because royalty used to have that color."

"I thought it meant that anyone with that coloring was considered ruling class," Elm said.

"It's rubbish." Evergreen poured himself more tea from the pot in the middle of the table.

"Of course it's rubbish," Robin said agreeably, "but Flame believes it. You'll like him, Rose. When he's not being obsessed with overthrowing the government, he can be awfully charming."

"Who's free tomorrow night?" Diamond asked. "We should introduce Rose to him."

Thirteen

Rose jerked from sleep at the sound of a gong going off under her head, or perhaps it only felt that way. She looked around at her room, gray in the pre-dawn light, but saw nothing out of place.

The gong sounded again, reverberating brassily until she could feel it in her bones and teeth. It wasn't unpleasant, just *loud*. She couldn't tell where it was coming from.

She looked out the window. The street was quiet. The gong sounded a third time and was followed by a chorus of crowing.

Oh, of course. It was a religious ceremony. Rose realized with dismay that it must happen every single morning at sunrise. No wonder the lodging house had had a room free.

She considered going back to sleep. Hopefully the gonging was finished. But she noticed her new easel and the nice big canvas she'd left on it.

She was awake, it was going to be a lovely morning, and she wanted to paint. She scrabbled around in the near-dark, grabbing her new paint tubes and shoving them into the travel kit by feel, then strapped the kit on under her belly. She pushed the window open and coasted out with the blank canvas in one paw and the easel in the other.

It was chilly out and the eastern sky was pale pink with dawn. Rose flapped slowly, awkward with her paws full and not sure where she was going. She listened to the sound of voices raised in a song she hadn't thought of since childhood and felt suddenly that she was very, very far from home.

She noticed a crooked lane a few streets over with a single dim light showing from one window. It was lantern light, not electric, but seemed bright in the darkness.

Rose dropped to the street and scurried back and forth for a few moments, trying to find just the right angle. The awning above the lighted window read "SILVER'S BAKERY."

She set up her easel finally, the lighted window just visible at an angle beyond the jutting corners of other buildings as the lane switched its way slightly downhill. The one light among all the dark buildings, with the faint sky framing uneven rooftops, was so impossibly perfect that Rose's paws trembled as she unbuckled her travel kit. She might not be able to capture this perfect moment—she might make a clumsy hash of it, ruin the canvas with an amateurish mess.

She made an irritated mewling sound when she opened her travel kit and realized it was still too dark to read the paint labels. She grabbed a piece of charcoal instead and sketched the building outlines on the canvas.

The light was strengthening so quickly that by the time she finished her sketch, she could read the paint tubes—*just*. She squirted colors on her palette to start with the sky.

She had so much experience painting skies now that it was easy to create a starry darkness just touched with dawn without laboring over it. She added burnt umber to her palette and painted the roofline, then roughed in the buildings.

She held the vision of the finished painting in her head and consulted her imagination for missing details as it grew lighter out. The street was dirt but she painted cobbles, because they gave texture to the foreground. When she painted the window's awning, she shortened the sign to just "BAKERY," which was easier to read.

She navigated the lighted window with caution, aware that this was where she could easily turn the painting into hackwork. She did not make it too bright: just a dim light, barely enough to faintly highlight the cobbles in front of the shop.

When she finished, it was almost what she had hoped. The crooked lane drew the eye to the lighted window, slightly off-center on the canvas. She added details to the buildings: a hint of brick and wood, door handles and hinges. But she wasn't satisfied with it.

The roofs, she decided. They needed to be brighter, emphasizing the dawn light. She also needed to lighten the sky on the dawn side of the canvas.

She did so, and the contrast of dragon-made light and the sky's light pulled the painting together so instantly that she caught her breath. She was done.

As often happened while she painted, Rose's entire attention was focused so intently that she forgot she had a body or that other people existed and could see her. She sat back, relaxing all at once, and saw a child watching her.

The girl was rosy-brown and very small, with bulky carry-bags over her back nearly as big as she was. "That's pretty," she said in a piping voice. "I never watched someone make a picture before. My name's Rose."

"My name's Rose too."

The small Rose gave a wriggle of excitement. "Where did you learn how to paint?"

"At school, I suppose. Shouldn't you be going along to school soon?"

"I'm not old enough. I have a job, though." Small Rose sounded proud. "I take newspapers to the kiosks."

Rose hadn't spent much time around small children and didn't know how to talk to this one. She said, "Better hurry, then. People will be wanting their morning papers soon."

"Will you be painting when I come back?"

"No, I'm done for now. I'm going to get breakfast."

"At the bakery?"

The bakery had opened at some point and people were going in and out. Rose said, "Maybe." Her stomach growled.

Small Rose giggled. "I have to go now."

Rose watched the child hurry away down the street, then glanced at her painting again.

It was still good. She signed it and wondered how on earth she would get it back to her room safely.

In the end, she hid her easel behind an overgrown hedge bordering someone's yard, and flew home with the painting. Once it was propped safely against the wall of her room, she returned for the easel. Then she spent a few minutes cleaning her brushes and washing paint from her paws before going in search of breakfast.

The bakery turned out to be larger than it looked from the front. It had a little space with tables and a modest menu of pastries and tea. The prices were much more reasonable than any she'd seen in Tirras so far.

Rose ordered a pot of tea and the "breakfast sampler," and settled at a table to eat and write in her travel journal.

It was still quite early and the bakery wasn't very busy, so Rose lingered. She felt content and full of quite good pastries when the small Rose pushed her way through the leather flaps over the front entrance.

The man behind the front counter said, "No beggars, I've told you before."

"She's barely out of the egg," said the woman working the café side of the shop. "We can give her a piece from the burnt batch."

"I'm not here to beg today," small Rose said. "I'm meeting a friend." She marched over to Rose's table.

Rose said to the woman behind the counter, "I'll feed her. I'd like another pot of tea anyway, and another of the almond scones for myself. What do you want, Rose?"

Small Rose sat across from her, squirming with excitement. Her carry-bags were empty. "I'd like an almond scone too!"

The woman brought small Rose a little clay bowl glazed blue, the hard-to-break kind young children needed, along with a fresh pot of tea. She pointedly set the teapot in front of grown Rose.

The child reached for the teapot. "No no, let me pour. It's heavy," Rose said. She poured and noted the steam rising from the bowl. "Don't burn your mouth."

Small Rose took a noisy slurp of tea. "Ooh, it's lovely!" she said in exaggeratedly refined tones, clearly imitating some adult. Rose watched her, bemused.

The woman returned with almond scones and a big chunk of bread, which small Rose grabbed. She took a giant bite and the woman immediately hooked it back out of her mouth. "Small bites. You'll choke."

She set a folded dishcloth next to grown Rose, who was baffled until small Rose knocked over her tea. Rose mopped it up and poured more, filling the bowl only halfway this time.

Fortunately, after that small Rose settled down to eat her bread without imperiling herself. She tried to talk while she ate until Rose said, "Don't talk with your mouth full."

When the bread was all eaten, small Rose sighed and said, "That was the best bread I ever ate."

"You still have your scone. Do you want me to tear it into pieces for you?"

"Yes please." Small Rose gave another wriggle and watched with pleasure as grown Rose carefully tore the flaky pastry into bite-sized pieces. Bits of icing and slivered almonds showered onto the plate.

"One bite at a time," Rose said, realizing as she spoke that she was echoing her own mother's words from long ago. "Swallow one before you take another."

From small Rose's delighted gasp when she tasted the scone, she wasn't used to such treats. "I never had anything like this!" she said. "It's so good!"

Rose ate her own scone and looked small Rose over. The girl was awfully young to be out without a minder. She was on the thin side too. "Do you live nearby?" Rose asked.

"On East Trillium Street."

"Is someone home to watch you when you get there?"

"Mama will be home mid-morning. Daddy goes to work when I do. We get up at the same time."

Rose glanced at the woman behind the counter, who was listening with her head ducked with concern. Rose felt the same way. Then she had to stop the child from licking slivers of icing off her plate.

Small Rose said, "What will you do with the painting you made?"

"Sell it to a rich lady."

The girl laughed. "Will you be rich too then?"

"Richer than I am now." Rose sketched the child in her travel journal, angling the book to hide what she was doing.

Small Rose noticed anyway. "What's that? Ooh, that's me! Can I have it?"

"No, I want to keep it. But I'll make a better drawing of you later that you can have." She caught her breath with excitement as an idea sprang to life. "Actually, I might make a painting of you, if your mother agrees."

"She'd love a painting of me!" small Rose said. "Will you make it now?"

"No, I need to talk to her first." Rose made another quick sketch of the girl, trying to capture in pencil lines the clumsy elegance of a child who kept moving.

She hadn't done a proper study of a model since school—landscapes were always more interesting. But trying new things was why she was in this strange bakery so far from home.

The bakery was starting to get busy, so Rose said, "Why don't you show me your favorite places, and when it's time for you to go home I'll come with you to talk with your mother."

Small Rose was happy to drag Rose around for the next two hours. The child showed her the best trees for climbing, good hiding spots, a butcher's where they made the best sausages, the kiosks where she delivered her newspapers, and the building where her best friend lived, "Only she's not at home right now. She goes to school."

Rose learned that small Rose's world was strictly bounded by certain streets she wasn't supposed to go past, and that she was too young to be able to fly yet. She also learned a great deal about the best friend, who was an older girl who came over to play with her after school. Small Rose had also decided to be an artist when she grew up. "I'll make paintings and sell them to rich ladies, and I will eat almond scones every day."

Rose thought suddenly how strange it was that a hungry child couldn't go in to any bakery or butcher's and ask for food, and be given it freely. What had gone wrong in draconic society that any child should be turned away with nothing? It was monstrous! At the same time, the more practical side of Rose understood that if a bakery gave away all its bread, the owners couldn't buy flour to make more. But it still seemed strange and wrong.

Rose said, "Why don't I buy some of those sausages as a gift for your parents? Come in and tell me your favorite kind."

Accordingly, when small Rose led the way to her lodgings, her carry-bags bulged with three different kinds of sausages, along with bread and a paper sack of almond scones from Silver's Bakery.

Small Rose's mother was the same pinky-brown as her daughter, and was remarkably lovely despite her obvious weariness. "I hope she hasn't been a nuisance," was the first thing she said, glancing guiltily from Rose to small Rose and back.

"No, not at all. She's a delight. I only came to talk to you."

"Oh. Come in, then—sorry for the mess. I never seem to have any time since they put me on night shift, even though I'm not working any more hours than before. Maybe it's energy I lack. How do you get so grubby, Rosie? You look like a piglet after a wallow."

Small Rose giggled and allowed her mother to give her a quick sponge from a ewer of water. Rose glanced around at the small room and thought no living space so bare could ever be called messy. The sleeping rugs were rumpled and a plate on the table was full of crumbs, that was all.

"There, that's got the top layer off, at least. Oh, I didn't say. I'm Briar."

Small Rose said, "She's named Rose too."

"Rose Blackthorn. Pleased to meet you."

"Would you like some tea?"

After walking what felt like several leagues that morning, Rose wanted a cup of tea desperately, but she hesitated. "I don't want to put you to any trouble."

"I was going to make one anyway. I've already filled the kettle." Briar lit the tiny iron stove with a match. "Don't keep interrupting, Rosie."

Small Rose had indeed tried repeatedly to break into the conversation. "But *Mama*, Rose is a painter! She's going to paint me!"

Briar glanced at Rose doubtfully. Rose said, "Only with your permission, of course, and naturally you'd be with us the whole time."

Small Rose said, "She bought us some *sausages*."

"A gift," Rose said, feeling awkward.

"And almond *scones*."

Briar said, "I'm sorry, I'm being very stupid right now. I don't understand."

Rose felt ridiculous suddenly. She sat down at the table with a thump and took out her journal. "I'm an artist. I would like Rose to be the subject of my next painting. I'd make one for you too, if you like." She flipped to the last page of the book, where she'd sketched the girl earlier. "I'd pay you for her time and yours."

Briar measured tea into a chipped yellow pot, her paws moving automatically while she herself blinked at Rose and her daughter in amazement. Rose suspected the woman's apparent vapidity was due to exhaustion.

Briar looked at the sketches and some of the tension in her attitude eased. "That's lovely. How wonderful it must be to be able to draw! Will she have to sit still for very long? She's not very good at that."

"No, just long enough for me to get a preliminary sketch."

"All right, then." Briar glanced around the room. "I usually have a sleep after my tea, but if you want to start now I can stay up."

"Not today," Rose said, aghast at the thought of making the poor woman remain awake one minute longer than necessary. Besides, the room had only one small window, which let in precious little light. "We can schedule for your day off—and I'd like to paint her outside, perhaps at a park."

Small Rose squirmed with delight. "May I? Mama, may I get my picture painted outside, *please*?"

They made plans over the tea, which was rather weak and unsweetened. Rose noticed how Briar's eyes kept trying to drift closed, and left as soon as she could do so without seeming rushed.

Fourteen

Rose painted two more canvases that day. One she made almost immediately after returning from meeting Briar, while her thoughts were still jolting from the thought of hatchlings going around hungry and unsupervised, to the equally unhappy thought of a young, beautiful woman working nights at a leather tannery and coming home worn out.

She painted from memory: the news kiosk next to a run-down greengrocer's, with the only figure a dragon standing behind the kiosk. Rose slashed paint onto the canvas as though trying to capture clouds on a windy day, hinting at details without trying to define them. It was very like painting the sky, she thought while she worked. In the end, everything was shape and texture and color.

The finished canvas would have horrified her old art teachers. She could practically hear them in her head, exclaiming over her lack of technique. But the memory of a student she had especially admired, a woman with a rough background and terrifying amounts of talent, stepped up and silenced the clamor. "That's good," the girl said in Rose's head, in tones of grudging admiration.

Rose said aloud, "I'm losing my mind." But she looked at her new work, the wet paint gleaming in the morning light, and decided it truly was good. She had captured the grim hopelessness of a man waiting for customers he knew would never come, but had done so without resorting to grays and browns. Instead, the painting was a riot of sharp highlights and deep, colorful shadows that implied a bright afternoon. Even the heap of rotting lettuces she'd added—to imply the smell she remembered from the day before—was green and dark red.

She propped the canvas next to the larger one she'd painted that morning. It looked drab in comparison, although still good.

"I can do anything," Rose thought, and collapsed on her bed and fell asleep.

Later that afternoon, after a quick lunch at the café across the street, she took her travel kit and went in search of the gong that had woken her that morning. She found it at the top of a small, steep hill just behind her lodging house, after she climbed a set of worn brick steps that drove directly through a thicket. The snarled vines and thorns arched above the path so that she had to keep her head down and her wings tightly folded. A long-legged dragon would need to nearly crawl. Then, when the sense of being trapped had nearly caused Rose to panic, the path opened into a grove of old, old trees. A gong nearly as tall as a dragon's length sat on a circle of bricks.

No one was around. Rose decided on a good angle to capture the gong gleaming in the dappled sun and shade, and opened her travel kit.

The subject was a bit predictable, so Rose concentrated on getting the light just right. She deepened the shadows, brightened the highlights. When she finished, her painted gong fairly glowed on the canvas, with patches of gold-tinted white between the maze of tree limbs and leaves implying a noonday sun.

The painting had taken much longer than the day's other works. By the time she was mostly satisfied with it, the sun was setting and shadows were genuinely taking over the grove. Rose packed up her kit carefully and strapped it on, then jumped into the air and pumped her wings hard to fly nearly straight up.

When she emerged above the trees, she realized the grove was exactly level with the upper floor of her lodging house, and not very far away from it. It took her less than a minute to fly home. No wonder the gong had woken her.

She set her new painting alongside the others. They were all very different but, she thought, very good. Before she cleaned her brushes, she added some details to the newest painting until she worried she would over-work it.

She was tired, but she also wanted to keep painting. It was as though a dam she'd not even known existed had broken at last, sending a torrent of ideas through her brain. But the light was going and she needed to get ready to meet Diamond and his group of friends.

Diamond's group met at a restaurant with a huge open patio. It was a warm night, the sky so full of stars that Rose could hardly tear her attention away from it. The patio was lit with strings of little glass lanterns that cast just enough light that diners could see their food and each other, while not outshining the sky.

Rose savored her meal of tender roast piglet and the local grain, which she'd learned was called rice, and thought about small Rose begging for burnt bread.

"You're quiet this evening," Diamond said. "Tired?"

"Yes, I was up early." Rose made an effort to brighten, and amused everyone by explaining about the gong. It was easy to be vague about where she was staying, since no one expected her to know her way around yet.

Evergreen wasn't with the group tonight, although the dragon named Flame was. He was a rich, dark pink speckled with yellow and royal red—a striking coloration Rose had never seen before. She'd been prepared to disdain him secretly, the way she disdained Evergreen, and was annoyed with herself that she found him so attractive.

Part of that was his personality. Flame paid close attention to anyone who spoke, as though he was impressed and trying to memorize their words. He also laughed easily.

Robin told him, with glee, about the character of Royal Red last night. "You'd have blown your bulb," she said, spreading the fingers of both front paws as though mimicking a lightbulb exploding.

Flame chuckled. "I'm immortal now—the subject of a comedic play."

"It doesn't bother you?" Elm asked.

"Of course not. They wouldn't make fun of me if I didn't threaten the status quo. They know change is coming, and they will resist it until they realize it's inevitable."

Rose wondered who "they" were: the playwright and actors, or the audience.

Flame turned his dark amber eyes on her. "This time next year—if not sooner—I will rule Tirras. I might rule all of North Stekka as well; that's my next goal."

"It sounds like a lot of work," Rose said, because she could think of nothing else to say.

Elm and Robin laughed. Crystal and Diamond looked at Flame as though curious about his reaction. Rose noticed that the people at nearby tables were obviously listening in too.

"I welcome hard work," Flame said. "I'm no figurehead. And of course I have no intention of deposing the current city officials, as long as they support me." He nodded regally to Elm, then said to Rose in a lower voice, "It would be good to have a companion's help."

"Like a deputy?" Rose asked, uncertain if she was misinterpreting his meaning.

Flame murmured, "Something more intimate."

The table fell silent. Rose couldn't breathe for a moment, pinned by Flame's intense gaze and the import of his words. She felt a flutter deep in her belly that had nothing to do with the meal.

"More tea, miss?" the server murmured.

Rose, profoundly glad for the interruption, said, "Oh yes, please. I'm parched."

Her mouth had gone dry, so the statement was quite true.

Elm changed the subject with a politician's easy grace, to Rose's relief. She felt off-balance and wanted time to think.

Once the group left the restaurant an hour or so later, Rose said her goodbyes hastily and took to the air. She flew not to her lodging house but higher and higher, soaring on a warm updraft that breathed across the city.

As she flew, she stared up at the night sky until the impossible depths and distances relaxed her. It was a beauty no artist could capture, the realm beyond even the sun and moon. She wondered if there were other dragons looking down at her as they winged from star to star. They must be strange and marvelous people.

Thoughtful and inspired, she sailed home and painted a dream-like landscape peopled with fanciful dragons: their wings long and elegant, their tails decorated with curling ribbons. The painted sky was spangled with stars, with the sun, moon, and a larger green sphere to represent Earth.

"Four paintings in one day," she thought, and fell asleep without cleaning her brushes.

Fifteen

The gong woke Rose at dawn. She startled from a sound sleep, disoriented, and staggered to the window in a vague panic. By the time she woke properly, the gong had sounded a third time and was replaced with dawn chorus crowing, then singing. Rose burrowed back into her blankets.

She dozed until morning light filled the room. Small Rose would probably expect to see her soon. She got up.

The first thing she saw was the fourth canvas she'd painted and the mess she'd left of her brushes and palette. She winced. Painting by candlelight had not helped her skill. The painting looked amateurish and unfinished, plus she had used far too much purple paint—the most expensive color, sold in tiny tubes and not always available at all.

She left it to worry about later and went to Silver's Bakery to wait for small Rose and buy her breakfast.

Rose had not intended to appoint herself small Rose's minder, but she felt a responsibility for the girl. After breakfast, she took her to see the gong and let her play in the quiet space among the tall trees while she sketched.

Once the girl was safely at home with her sleepy mother, Rose turned her attention—reluctantly—to yesterday's paintings.

What had seemed brilliant yesterday, even borderline genius, now embarrassed her. Every painting was different, with no cohesion of style. She had not been so scattered since art school. Taken individually, each painting was good enough, or would be once finished. Taken together...well, she would not let anyone see them together.

She filled her travel kit's tiny cup with turpentine and poked a brush at the purple she'd left on her palette. She would finish that painting and hang it on the wall once it dried. At least she'd only used her smallest canvas.

Morning sun filled the room, giving her good light to work by. Rose defined the painting's figures against the background, added blues and pinks to make it less overwhelmingly *purple*, used some green in the foreground to echo the green of Earth. When she decided it was finished, it was a much better painting, although still not anything like her usual style. It was cute, though, like an illustration from a storybook. Perhaps small Rose might like it.

Later, while she ate at the café across the street, she got the idea for a new painting. She could paint the beginning of a race without it seeming saccharine if she only depicted the flyers' wings during take-off. It would be a challenge of composition to obscure all the faces without it seeming contrived, and she would need to imply a great deal of movement in a static image.

She grew so interested in her initial sketch that she forgot to drink her tea until it was stone cold. She ordered a fresh pot.

When she returned to her room, she redid the sketch on a canvas. It took an hour to get it just the way she wanted it. Then she prepared her palette—with no purple at all this time—took a deep breath, and started painting.

She worked as fast as possible, slashing paint onto the canvas as she'd done with her newspaper seller yesterday. Only pieces of a pale blue sky were visible between the maze of lifted wings of all colors, although she thinned her paints when depicting the wings' membranes. It made them appear as though bright light was shining through them. She deepened the shadows under bellies and tails to help the illusion of a bright afternoon.

It took her less time to finish the painting than it had to make the sketch. She was pleased with the result. It matched her newspaper seller piece, too, so at least she wasn't haring off into yet another direction with her style.

As she cleaned her brushes and palette, Rose realized what was happening. "I'm growing," she said aloud. "That's why I took this rotten trip, so I shouldn't complain, but I wish it wasn't happening all at once."

She wished also that she had someone to talk to about it. She missed Honey, who would evaluate the paintings quietly and give her an honest critique and advice.

That reminded her suddenly of Oriole Sky. She had Honey's letter of introduction but no idea where to find the artist. Somewhere in the mountains, that's all she knew.

Dawn might know, and Rose needed to talk to Dawn anyway.

"I don't think she lives very close to Tirras," Dawn said when Rose asked. "They'd know at her gallery on Elmwood Circle; check there. Your other painting sold, by the way. It wasn't even on display yet. Word about you is getting out."

Rose sat back on her haunches, disconcerted. "Really?"

"Yes. You seem to be running with quite the crowd already." Dawn gave her a steady look.

Rose suspected that under her placid demeanor, Dawn was more of a firebrand than Flame—who was probably all hot air anyway. For a moment Rose wanted to apologize for meeting Diamond and getting caught up in a group of people she didn't like very much.

The shop was empty at the moment. Rose decided she needed to talk about her confusion, and Dawn was likely to be sympathetic. "I'm staying in Green," she said. "There's a little girl, too young to fly, with a job although she's not even old enough for school, and unsupervised half the morning, and too thin, and I've been making sure she gets breakfast, at least. And then in the evening I fly up to Pink and meet a lot of very rich dragons who think nothing of spending more money on a single meal than the girl's parents probably make in a year. And because I know those dragons, my paintings sell for really ridiculous prices."

Her jumble of words barely made sense. Rose fell silent and waited for Dawn's reaction.

Dawn nodded and, Rose thought, relaxed a fraction. "Welcome to Tirras. I think of leaving all the time, but if all the people with a conscience leave, who will help those who are struggling and can't relocate? I do a lot of volunteer work."

"Can I help?"

"Yes, of course."

They discussed it for a while, between customers. Rose pretended to be the shop assistant again and helped wrap up paintings when they sold.

Rose explained too about her plan to paint small Rose's portrait. "Her mother suggested the local park, but I took a look at it earlier and it's all trampled dirt and the backs of buildings. There's hardly any green. I need her to stand out against a really lush background."

"Bring her and her parents up to Blue; we have some lovely parks. I'll meet you with my boys and we'll make a picnic of it."

Rose left, feeling much better about things, and went to find Elmwood Circle.

When she entered the large and attractive Skybird Studio soon after, she was stunned. The gallery was full of paintings, large and small. Oriole's landscapes were so realistic that Rose felt they were windows, not canvases, but the slant of light and shadow evoked emotions beyond mere admiration. Rose stared first at a huge painting of mountains, where nothing about it *specifically* said "winter" but which nevertheless was a winter scene. She turned next to a deceptively simple depiction of a flower-filled meadow, then a painting of a narrow creek switching its way through dry-looking trees, with the impressions of many paw- and hoof-prints in the mud along its edges.

Rose wandered through the gallery, feasting on the works of an artist at the pinnacle of her power. When she finally realized she'd been looking at paintings for at least an hour, she felt buoyed by inspiration like a warm updraft under her wings.

When she came up to the counter, the clerk said impatiently, "We're not a museum, you know."

Rose only just stopped her wings from mantling. She decided to be haughty in return. "I have a letter of introduction to Oriole Sky. I was told you could tell me where she lives."

The woman gave a disbelieving huff. "I think not."

Rose had fortunately brought the letter with her, sealed in a high-quality envelope with Honey's neat handwriting on the front. "Perhaps I can send this to her care of you," she said icily. "I'll write my contact information on the front." She found a pencil in her bag and wrote "Rose Blackthorn, Sunny Garden Gallery" in bold letters.

The woman looked startled. "Yes, of course," she said in more ingratiating tones. "I'm sorry for misunderstanding you."

All the enjoyment of art had fled from Rose, leaving anger and a certain amount of self-loathing behind. How vile that after only a few days in Tirras, she was already using her name to get her way. How unpleasant that she needed to.

The next morning, when Rose dropped small Rose off at home, she explained about a picnic in Blue to Briar.

"Oh, that does sound lovely," Briar said with longing in her voice. "I don't think I've flown that far since I laid Rose's egg."

"What's a picnic?" small Rose asked, and was speechless with joy at the answer.

Accordingly, Rose arranged for a picnic hamper, which Dawn said she would pick up and bring to the park with her two foster-ling sons. She also said her sons could carry canvases and easel for her.

The morning of the picnic was overcast, which concerned Rose. If it rained, they would need to wait another two weeks until both of small Rose's parents had a day off. But the clouds had mostly blown away by the time they'd arranged to meet.

Rose had not yet met small Rose's father, Stone, who worked in a sawmill on the edge of the city. He was a slender, wiry dragon, pale brown with an attractive pattern of black splotches along his sides and rings down his tail. He was missing two fingers.

The family's small room was spotless when Rose arrived, and Stone carried a large leather bag stuffed with items they might need—as though they'd be gone for days instead of hours. Small Rose was nearly galloping around the room in excitement.

"Ready?" Rose asked, catching the holiday feeling off the family. "Follow me!"

The adults jumped into the air, and Stone swung down to pick up his daughter around her middle. "Oof! You're getting so heavy and grown up!" he said, and small Rose laughed in his arms.

The morning air was fresh and warm, promising a hot day. Stone and Briar took turns carrying their daughter, encouraging her to spread her wings and practice flapping them. She squealed with excitement whenever the wind caught under them.

Rose set a slow pace, so they arrived at the park without anyone being too tired. Dawn was already there. She had spread a blanket on the grass and was lounging on it, a huge picnic basket on one side and Rose's easel and blank canvases on the other.

Rose's stomach fluttered with nerves as she landed. She wasn't really a portraitist. What if she did a terrible job?

Dawn called her two sons over from where they were playing in a shallow creek. They were older than small Rose and, the elder explained to the girl, they had the day off school as a special treat so they could meet her.

Small Rose, overcome with excitement, looked up at her mother and gasped, "Is it my hatchday?"

Briar nuzzled her daughter. "Close enough. Go play for a bit."

"Tire yourself out," Stone said with a laugh. "Remember Auntie Rose needs you to sit for her soon."

Rose, both delighted and alarmed at being elevated to honorary auntie, took out her new sketchbook with trembling paws. She wished she had not decided to paint a portrait. But the sight of small Rose leaping and tumbling with Dawn's boys, and Briar and Stone relaxing together in the dappled shade, made her glad she had arranged this moment of joy for the family.

Rose filled several pages with sketches: of small Rose, of the boys, of the creek and trees—everything in sight. She felt her nerves and paws steady.

She noticed after a while that Briar had fallen asleep in the grass. Stone was watching her sleep with such tenderness in his expression that Rose glanced away, embarrassed at intruding. Then she sketched the pair quickly.

Dawn noticed and gave her an amused look. Dawn had a sketchbook out too, and Rose was delighted to learn that the gallery owner was a good artist in her own right, with a deliberate style very different from Rose's. She was mostly drawing her own boys.

Finally, Rose decided it was time to paint. She set up her easel and prepared her palette. Perhaps she should start with a simple landscape.

Small Rose noticed the easel, though, and bounded over to say breathlessly, "Is it time?"

"I suppose so," Rose said, anxiety surging again. "Can you sit still for a few minutes while I get a sketch of you?"

Small Rose sat obligingly, and Rose decided her natural posture was better than a more studied pose. She drew the girl quickly on paper, then again on the canvas with a piece of charcoal. Then, paws shaking again, she picked up her brush.

She roughed in the background first, as fast as she could, aware that small Rose would start squirming soon. Then she grabbed another brush and, heart hammering, smoothed on the first stroke of umber.

By the time small Rose started to fidget, Rose had the shape of the girl on canvas, although with no details yet. "That's all for now. Go play some more."

Small Rose came around the easel. "That doesn't look much like me."

"It doesn't yet," Rose agreed. "Paintings are always made back to front. I did the sky and trees and the ground behind you first, and now I'm painting you, and then I'll add the foreground—that's the bit in front of you. Lastly I'll go back and put details in to make it look real."

Small Rose said, "Will you put a bird in too? Can I have a bird sitting on my head?"

Dawn and Stone both laughed. Briar stirred in her sleep.

"I'll add a bird if you can get one to sit on your head," Rose said.

Small Rose tore off toward the creek, where Dawn's boys were building a fort out of stones. "Help me catch a bird!"

Rose laughed too, suddenly confident. It was a lovely day and she had lots of canvases. If this one didn't turn out well, she'd try again.

Sixteen

The portrait turned out well. The girl in her painting looked like small Rose—the artless pose charming, her underdeveloped wings indicating her young age. Rose attributed this success to luck, although she didn't say so. But her use of light and shadow to indicate a sunny spring morning, her rendition of the trees arching over the girl and the sky visible through them: that was skill.

Last of all, Rose added faint shadows along the girl's side to indicate her ribs showing more than they should. It was barely noticeable.

Dawn was watching her paint, although Rose had as usual forgotten that a world and other people existed outside of her canvas. She only remembered when she heard Dawn give a quick little catch of breath.

"Is that good, do you think?" Rose murmured.

"It's the most important detail."

"I think I'm done."

Stone woke Briar and they both admired the painting. "It's marvelous," Briar said. "It looks just like her! I wish I could afford to buy it."

"I'm making one just for you next," Rose said. "It'll be a different pose, that's all."

Dawn said, "Let's eat first. I'm getting hungry and I expect the children are ravenous after all their playing."

After the picnic, Rose painted a second portrait of small Rose for her parents. She depicted the girl laughing with a sparrow perched on her head, and didn't accentuate her ribs.

Briar and Stone were delighted, as was small Rose. Rose herself felt she could do anything, since the second painting had turned out as well as the first. Luck could not have struck twice. It must be skill after all.

"It'll take a week or so to dry properly," Rose said. "Once it's dry, I'll get it framed for you and you can hang it up."

"Thank you so much," Briar said, her voice rough with emotion. "This has been the best day I can remember in years."

Dawn said, "I have your daughter's sitting fee here." She handed a pouch full of coins to Briar. "Would you like to see the gallery before you head home? It's not far."

With the boys helping carry everything, they flew to the Sunny Garden Gallery. The shop assistant was on duty, and to Rose's dismay, Evergreen and his grandmother were there too.

Dawn made a very quiet disapproving sound in her throat. "I'll just run these upstairs so they can dry," she said, and carefully held the paintings so that the visitors couldn't see them.

Evergreen's grandmother said in her demanding voice, "I must see them first."

Dawn turned them around reluctantly. "They're not for sale."

The grandmother looked at the portraits, then at small Rose staring around in wonder, then at the girl's parents. "You've chosen a really delightful portraitist," she said to Briar. "I have one of her pieces too. I didn't realize she took commissions."

Briar nodded, apparently overcome. The grandmother turned to Dawn and said, "Could you ask the artist to contact me? I'd like to commission her."

Evergreen cleared his throat and said in a deferential voice—quite unlike his usual tone, "Rose Blackthorn is right here, Grandmother. She helps out at the gallery sometimes for fun, I believe."

Rose caught his eye and glared. She didn't know how to say no to his grandmother. Maybe Dawn would come up with something.

The grandmother said, "I'm so glad to meet you. You're a rising star, from what I keep hearing. I'd like my portrait painted, as a gift to my family."

Dawn murmured, "This is Beryl Tirras. Her family founded this city many generations ago."

Beryl said, "When can you start?"

That night at a post-concert meal, Evergreen had everyone in hysterics explaining the situation. "You should have seen Rose's *face*," he said. "She looked like she wanted to murder me."

"I certainly didn't," Rose said, unamused. "I'm just not a very good portrait painter. Besides, how do I keep from making her look old? She won't like that, but I can't pretend I see her as young."

Evergreen said, "She said she wanted the portrait as a *gift to her family*. I almost laughed out loud."

Robin snickered. "You mean you won't cherish it when she leaves it to you in her will?"

"I'll only cherish it because that means she's dead. Then I'll burn it."

"You will not," Rose said. "Give it back to me." Everyone laughed.

"Will you paint *my* portrait?" Flame asked. "I can pay you in *so* many ways."

Everyone laughed again. Rose made a mockery of her own emotions and hid her face in her wing, prompting even more laughter.

The next morning, after she had escorted small Rose home, full of almond scones and tea, Rose met Dawn and a young man hired to help carry equipment. Dawn had negotiated Beryl's fee—which was astronomical—and managed to wangle a tour of all the art too. For this Dawn would be paid, since she was cataloging the collection.

The house was even more astounding than Rose had imagined. It was built of white stone with huge sculpted gardens all around it and a sweeping view of Tirras. A pair of guards flew out to escort them to the entrance.

Rose met Beryl in a beautifully appointed morning room, and was glad Evergreen was nowhere to be seen. Beryl was almost giddy with excitement. "I can't decide if I want my portrait done inside or out. I thought this room would make a good background, but perhaps it's too dark."

"Outside," Rose said, horrified at the thought of having to render realistic curtains in the long windows or the geometric designs carved on the wall panels. "Show me your favorite part of the gardens and we'll find a good angle."

"What a lovely idea! I know just the spot."

Beryl chose a pond surrounded by willow trees. This surprised Rose, who expected to have to paint trimmed hedges and angular flowerbeds. The pond was mostly wild. Willow fronds trailed in the water and occasionally a big goldfish nosed the surface. Frogs and birds called.

"This is perfect," Rose said. "Just here, I think, so the branches hang down behind you."

"What sort of pose would be best?" Beryl asked.

"It depends on what emotion you want to convey," Rose said, remembering a long-ago lecture on portraits. She had barely paid attention at the time and was glad that particular wisdom had stuck.

Beryl looked around. "I think...I'd like to appear natural. As myself. It's for my family, you know. If I'm looking straight out of the painting, it would make me resemble a banker."

Rose laughed. The old woman seemed likable suddenly. Rose hoped her other family members were more fond of her than Evergreen was.

Beryl sat next to the pond, looking down at the water as though entranced with the fish. Rose hastily grabbed her sketchbook while Dawn set up the easel and large canvas.

The pose was a good one: it happened to be an easy pose to paint, and for Beryl to hold for a long time without growing uncomfortable.

Beryl didn't fidget like small Rose, but she did talk. Fortunately she didn't seem to mind that Rose's replies were vague and distracted.

"My landscaper wanted to put a gazebo next to this pond, but I thought it didn't need anything artificial. Don't you think? Sometimes nature needs no help. The rest of the grounds are what people expect, because of course the house isn't just mine, it's my family's. But this pond is all for me. I suppose that sounds conceited."

"Not at all," Rose said, concentrating on the curve of Beryl's tail where it lay across the flower-spangled grass.

"I love it best in winter, strange to say. It gets cold here and sometimes when I come out in the mornings, there's ice on the water. But I can see my fish moving around near the bottom. It always reminds me of life in the egg. I'm not much given to poetics, but it feels profound."

Rose roughed in the foreground. "How many children do you have?"

"Four, and nine grandchildren." Beryl sounded proud. "It's wonderful to be part of a large family. The children squabble, of course, but they're all quite fond of each other underneath it. I was an only child and it was quite lonely, so I wanted to make sure that wouldn't happen to my children."

Beryl told her all about her family, none of which Rose remembered for more than a few seconds. She was painting more slowly now, adding details that were easy to get wrong: light and shadow, the ripples on water, the shadowy forms of fish.

After a while, Rose said, "You can move now if you like."

Beryl unfroze and stretched. "Skies, that feels good. May I peek?"

"Not quite yet, if you don't mind."

"Then I'll lie down and rest."

Beryl did so and promptly fell asleep. Rose was able to work in peace for a while.

The painting was more elaborate than yesterday's, what with the willow fronds, fish, flowers, and reflections in water. It took Rose much longer than she expected to finish it. She felt her energy flagging long before she was satisfied with the piece.

Annoyed that Beryl was sleeping so peacefully, Rose added the suggestion of a hollow behind the hip bone, extra definition of shadows on the face that implied age. Somehow the small details added up and made the figure look much more like Beryl, and much older than Rose had intended—but no older than Beryl actually appeared.

By the time Beryl sat up and yawned, Rose was famished and exhausted. She needed a latrine too. She said, "I think I'm done for now. I want to make some changes tomorrow, but I can do that at the studio. It's mostly done." She hesitated and turned the painting around, her stomach clenching with nerves. "What do you think?"

Beryl looked for a long time without comment. Rose couldn't read her expression. Finally the woman said, "It's me, isn't it? Just as I wanted. Do I really look...so old?"

Rose stammered, so unsure of what to say that she could make no words at all beyond, "Uh, uh, may—um."

Beryl interrupted her. "Never mind. There's no answer to that question. Of course I'm not young anymore, and it's absurd to expect flattery from honest art. You've painted me as I truly am, and if I'm old, you've also taken care to show I still retain some beauty."

"Oh, you're definitely still beautiful!" Rose said, shaky with relief. It was true, for that matter. Beryl must have been a stunner in her day.

"You've included two of my fish," Beryl said more warmly. "Thank you. They can live almost as long as a dragon, you know. I've had them for decades."

Beryl insisted that Rose stay for lunch. They ate in a sunny room overlooking the gardens, and even the fine restaurant fare Rose had been eating lately didn't compare to the perfection of the meal. It finished with a honey cake decorated with sugared flowers and icing bees, so sumptuous that Rose closed her eyes at every bite, determined to savor every morsel.

By now Rose knew that the huge house wasn't Beryl's alone, that all her children and most of her grandchildren lived there. But no one joined them for lunch.

Seventeen

The next several weeks fell into a routine as odd as any Rose had ever experienced. She started waking naturally before the gong went, and finally joined the small congregation for the ceremony. It was a ragged little group, mostly elderly dragons but a few younger ones, all of them earnest and welcoming of a new member. Rose found she enjoyed the simple ceremony, especially the singing.

After that she met small Rose for breakfast at Silver's Bakery, then took the girl to the minder Briar had arranged with the sitting fee. The minder was an elderly woman with a trampled yard full of tiny children and a great many toys, and Rose was delighted to learn that it included a mid-morning snack, lunch, then a nap, and then crafts and lessons designed for preschool children. Within two weeks small Rose had become healthily plump.

Rose spent the morning painting, took lunch somewhere in Green, painted some more if she had an idea or sketched and doodled if she didn't. Then she met Dawn and her boys for volunteer work after school let out. Some days they helped make bread and soup to serve to those who couldn't afford food, some days they took care packages to elderly or infirm dragons and helped clean their homes, some days they delivered storybooks and snacks to children whose families couldn't afford such luxuries. It was exhausting, because Rose felt the problems in Tirras were so large that her small efforts were barely noticeable, but it was rewarding too.

And after that, most evenings she spent with Diamond and his group of friends, wasting a sickening amount of money on restaurants and entertainment.

Rose wasn't sure why she kept joining the group. She told herself it was because they were influential, and her paintings were selling as fast as she could finish them as a result. She told herself also that she needed to see the contrast of rich and poor lest she become jaded during her volunteer work. But she worried, usually during her night flights home to Green, that she only liked the notoriety and luxury.

Spring shaded into early summer. One day she stopped by the gallery and Dawn handed her an envelope.

Rose ripped it open, mystified. She didn't recognize the handwriting.

"Oh! It's from Oriole Sky." Rose scanned the letter. "She wants me to visit!"

"When will you go?" Dawn asked.

"Soon, I expect. I need to make some arrangements first."

"Paint me some more sky studies before you go."

Rose took her easel and a canvas to Silver's Bakery and set it up across the street. She had a more important painting to make first.

She painted the bakery carefully, taking care to make it look precisely realistic and yet *moreso*, a brighter, cleaner version of itself. The big square door was propped open in her picture, although the bakery was actually closed for the afternoon, and several figures were visible through the front window. It looked cheerful, busy, welcoming.

It didn't take long and she took the painting home to dry, pleased that she had thought of it. She scrubbed paint off her paws, then took the purple star-dragon painting she'd made weeks ago to be framed. Then she returned home to get ready for the evening.

She was prepared, when she met Diamond and his group, to explain that she was leaving Tirras. She would stay with Oriole for a while, then continue her journey into South Stekka.

The thought of leaving Tirras filled her with relief. It was long past time to go.

But when she joined her usual group at the plaza near Diamond's bank, Diamond was talking passionately of the seaside. Seeing him passionate about anything was astonishing in itself, since he was the most reserved and calculating dragon she had ever met. The group revolved around him, or rather he stood in the middle, manipulating everyone who came near—not in a malicious way, but ruthless nevertheless. Rose could not understand him. She had seen one pretty young woman join the group, brought along by Elm, and just as quickly be shunted out and never invited again. When Rose asked Diamond about her, he had replied, "Her father is rather a bore" as though that explained everything.

Rose had also given up wondering where Diamond got the money to finance his evenings out. He was only a banker. She had imagined he was stealing from the bank somehow, then wondered if he was blackmailing rich people. Ultimately she decided he simply knew how to invest his pay and was living well off the interest.

Now, though, Diamond was as animated as Robin in front of an audience. "We'll fly down at the end of the week, and anyone who can't come will just have to join us later. Rose! Are you coming to the seaside with us?"

"No, I can't. I'm going to visit Oriole Sky."

Ordinarily, Diamond could be counted on to tuck that sort of information away for later use. He knew all the most important people in Tirras, and their business. But tonight he said, "Bother Oriole Sky. You can see her anytime. Come with us!"

Elm said with exaggerated seriousness, "Diamond will teach you how to fish."

At this, Diamond's pale hide flushed faintly pink with excitement. "Of course! Everyone should know how to fish. It's really quite the most important skill one can learn, along with cooking fish. And you should learn how to start a fire without matches. Unless you know already?"

"No," Rose said. "I'd never have taken you for a fisher."

"Oh, skies." Diamond clapped his paws together in agitation. "Fishing is the most important skill, I tell you. Oh, I wish we were flying there now!"

Seeing Diamond like this was so interesting that Rose decided to postpone her visit to Oriole. "All right, I'll join you. Who else is coming?"

Elm said, "I am, and I'm sure Robin will. She always enjoys it."

"I am too," Flame said, "although I can't promise I can stay the whole two weeks. I have irons in the fire, you know."

Rose no longer took Flame seriously. He was handsome and clever, but his obsession with bloodlines and royal red was tiresome, and Rose had seen no indication that he did anything practical with his time. Still, her egg months were almost over, and he had made it amply clear that he wanted her as a lover.

Rose painted several sky studies over the next few days, along with some nice if not especially inspired landscapes. Because her paintings were selling so well, and for such high prices, Rose felt she should keep painting as much as possible—but, she thought, she badly needed a break. She no longer had time to do much experimenting, the way she had done when she first arrived in Tirras.

The day before she left for the seaside, she took the framed star-dragon painting to small Rose. It was her parents' day off and they were in the middle of packing a modest picnic while small Rose danced about with excitement.

"Auntie Rose! Are you coming too?"

"Oof!" Rose gave the girl a quick hug with her wings. "No, but I brought you something. It's a painting just for you."

Small Rose gasped. "Purple is my favorite color!"

"It's a painting of the dragons that live among the stars. And I'm sorry to say it has to be a goodbye present. I'm leaving tomorrow."

"When will you be back?"

Rose had to clear her throat twice. "Never. I'm going to visit South Stekka and then I'm going to make my way home to Dayrill."

Small Rose started to wail. Rose hugged her again, unable to speak.

Eighteen

The last thing Rose did before she left was take her painting of Silver's Bakery, now framed, to the bakery itself. She gave it to the owners in exchange for them feeding small Rose breakfast every morning until she started school.

Then she flew to Pink and joined Diamond, Flame, Robin, Elm, and Crystal.

It was barely past dawn. Rose had bought a sackful of scones at the bakery and passed them out to her friends now. "Is Evergreen not coming?" she asked, secretly hoping he wasn't.

"His grandmother wants him for some rearranging," Crystal said. "He's hoping to get away in a few days."

Diamond, who was wearing a small leather pack, opened his wings. "Less talking, more flying."

"I'm not done with my scone," Robin said. "This is good, Rose. Where did you find it?"

"Just a little bakery near my lodging house," Rose said.

Elm laughed. "Afraid we'll come buy up all the scones if you tell us where it is?"

"Yes. It's quite a small place."

They flew toward the dark western horizon. Rose had done plenty of flying while in Tirras, since the city was so spread out, but she hadn't done much long-distance flying. By the time they landed for lunch at a village nestled among the western foothills, she was nearly as tired as everyone else. Only Diamond didn't complain, although he bolted his food eagerly and drank half a pot of tea in minutes.

After that, though, the hills were less steep. The mountains receded behind them until they were blue in the distance. The horizon was perfectly flat.

"We're almost there!" Diamond called over his back, his near-white wings pumping steadily in the still afternoon air.

Rose took the flat horizon to mean there was a big lake ahead, even though she knew it was the ocean. It looked like Lake Inga at home, where her family had vacationed occasionally. As they flew closer, she saw green-blue water stretching as far as she could see.

It was stupendous, as awesome in its way as her first view of the mountains—but much less alarming since she had food and friends with her. When they reached the coast at last and Rose saw waves crashing on the sand, she wanted to crow with joy as though the sun had just risen after a hard night.

Diamond soared in a broad arc that brought him over the water, then down to a half-moon of sand behind a row of dunes and in front of some trees. A break in the dunes led to the small open space, and as she followed Diamond, Rose noticed a shack humbler than any in Green.

Diamond dropped to the ground in front of the shack. "Home sweet home!" he called as the others landed too, in various states of exhaustion. "Let's see how it fared the winter storms."

Rose followed him in, although the others stayed outside, groaning and complaining that their wings ached. There was only a single room with a hard-packed sand floor and a small fire pit in the middle. It smelled musty and Rose helped Diamond unboard the windows and fling them open for fresh air.

Diamond was like a different person. He rushed here and there, making things cozy: spreading out his sleeping blanket, hanging a set of cooking utensils on a wall hook, retrieving pieces of driftwood from a pile near the door and laying out a fire for later.

"Let's see if we can catch a nice big fish for our supper," he said to Rose, his eyes bright. "Want to learn how to fish?"

"Why not?" Rose said.

She had seen people fishing on the lake, sweeping low over the water to snag them from the surface. She had never tried, content to let her parents buy fish already caught.

Diamond made shooing motions with his wings at the others. "Go gather driftwood, you layabouts! You have to work if you want to eat."

Robin had flopped onto her side in the coarse grass. "Have pity! We're all worn out."

"The sea air will revive you. Rose and I are going fishing."

Rose was glad that her energy had returned, although her wing muscles did protest when she took off again. She and Diamond flapped over the dunes and Rose felt the gusty ocean breeze buoy her. It tasted of salt.

She flew close to Diamond to hear his shouted instructions over the crashing surf. "We want a good-sized fish. I'll dive for it, you grab its tail when I haul it up."

Rose wondered how she could do that without colliding with him and sending them both plummeting into the water. But she could swim well enough to get to shore if necessary.

They coasted over the water. Sea birds squawked in alarm and flew away. Rose saw larger birds in the distance, their long, narrow wings white against the sky as they swooped and dived.

Diamond led her far past the swelling waves, their tops laced with foam, to choppier, greener water. He flew with his front legs hanging, fingers flexed like a hawk's claws. "There!" he shouted suddenly. "See them?"

Rose saw shadows below the surface and the silvery glint of sun off scales. There were half a dozen large fish, widely spaced, chasing a school of smaller ones.

"Can you lift a fish that size?" Rose called back, aghast.

"Oh yes, it's just a matter of getting a good grip."

Diamond angled his wings for a dive, his front legs extended. Rose watched, terrified for him.

His legs hit the water with a splash at the same time that he pulled out of his dive. He pumped his wings hard and heaved one of the great fish out of the sea, his claws buried in its gills on either side.

Rose saw instantly when he meant about grabbing the tail. She soared below him and hooked her own claws into the thrashing tail, beating her wings shallowly so they wouldn't dip into the water and unbalance her. She thought suddenly of the duck race back in Inkle.

She looked up and saw Diamond crush the fish's head in his jaws—a savage bite that sent the fish into a frenzy before its movement stilled into twitching.

"I've got it now," he called. Rose let go and sailed away, following him toward shore.

She saw the others picking up driftwood up and down the beach, moving in a desultory way. Flame's bright coloration stood out against the sand like a live coal.

Elm glanced up. Rose couldn't hear what he said, but the others all looked up too. Their cheering sounded like gulls crying across the water.

Diamond flew not to the shack but down the coast a short distance, where the dunes started farther back from the beach. In the loose sand at their base Rose saw a larger fire pit with enough room around it for everyone to lounge. A stream trickled between the dunes nearby and into the ocean.

Diamond landed carefully, flapping hard to slow before dropping to his hind legs next to the fire pit. He set the fish on the sand and stood over it, blood on his jaws and paws.

Rose landed and stared at him in wonder. She had never considered Diamond particularly attractive or interesting, but suddenly she saw him in new light. He looked like a wild dragon from the olden days, strong and capable.

He started digging sand out of the half-buried fire pit and Rose hurried to help. "That was first rate!" she said. "You made it look easy."

"It was mostly luck." He used a pawful of sand to scrub fish blood off his jaws. "The bluetails are common off the coast this time of year, but not usually so close to shore. You did well helping me, thanks."

Rose felt as proud as though she had snagged the fish herself.

The others came hurrying up the beach with carry-bags full of driftwood. The fish was duly admired and Crystal, who was smallest, lay down beside it so they could compare sizes. "It's almost exactly your length, not counting your tail," Robin said.

The fire pit was big enough to hold several such fish. Diamond jumped down into it and arranged the driftwood, then used a stick and a length of dried kelp to start a fire without matches, with a lot of dry seaweed as kindling. His movements were so sure that Rose marveled again—not at the fire, although it was impressive that he could conjure it without matches or flint, but at his transformation from urbane banker to a dragon of the wild.

Once the driftwood was alight, spitting blue flames from salt, Diamond climbed out of the pit but stayed to feed the fire from above. He sent Rose and the others to gather more wood.

When Rose returned, flying so she could carry her armload of driftwood more easily, the fire was burning low. Diamond said, "We want a bed of good coals to lay the fish on. Too hot and the meat will burn. Have you gutted a fish before?"

"Skies, no," Rose said, sitting back and dusting sand from her paws. "Why on earth should I have?"

"It's a useful skill. I'll show you how."

"No, really, you needn't."

Diamond sliced the fish's belly open with a claw, a messy procedure that took a minute or so. Rose watched in horror at the operation that followed.

"I won't save the offal tonight," he said, scooping it into a messy heap. "Tomorrow, perhaps, I'll show you how to use it to catch sharks, but we have plenty to eat right now."

By the time the others returned with more wood, Diamond pronounced the coals just right. He lay the fish on them carefully, then used a flat piece of wood to shovel more coals into its body cavity and over it.

Crystal said, "Must you leave fish guts lying around, Diamond? It's really almost too much."

"You're capable of moving them yourself."

"No thanks! I have to eat with these paws later."

"As if you didn't have an entire ocean to wash in," Diamond said, and they all laughed.

Since Diamond was busy prodding the coals with a long stick, and no one else seemed interested in cleaning up, Rose scooped the offal up and carried it out to sea to drop it. When she returned, Crystal had fetched a jug from somewhere and was busy juicing a huge bag of oranges into it.

Rose said, "No wonder you're tired, if you carried all those oranges."

"Elm carried them, but I had the jug and juicer."

Elm said, "Worth the trouble, I think, although after tonight we'll have to pick our own oranges."

"Do they grow on trees or bushes?" Rose asked, and the others laughed—not unkindly.

"Trees, a bit inland," Robin said. "It's still early for other fruit but last year the peaches were already ripe when we got here."

Flame returned from filling a big teakettle at the stream and plunked it on the hot coals. "Hot water, coming up. Who brought bowls?"

That first night on the seaside was near-perfection. They had hot tea mixed with orange juice and enough delicate, flaky fish that everyone gorged on it and there was still more to nibble on. The heat from the fire pit offset the chill of the breeze as sunset advanced, gilding the ocean orange and pink at first, then shadowed purple.

Someone started singing "The Last Little Cloud" and they all joined in. On the chorus, Rose laughed so hard at hearing a lot of adults singing the "wee-wee-wee-wee-*rain*" that she could barely breathe. After that they sang "New Year's Dance," "My Lover's Wings," and a dozen more, until the last glint of sunlight was long gone and the moon shone on the placid ocean.

Rose lay between Flame and Crystal. When she grew sleepy, Rose rested her head against Flame's warm side. She could hear his breathing. She tried to remember when, precisely, her egg months

were over. Soon, she knew: but she had thrown out her little card
ages ago when it was obvious she wasn't growing an egg.

Nineteen

Over the next week, Rose learned how to harvest oranges and other fruit, how to catch a fish and bite its life out, how to start a fire without matches, and how to cook fish of various kinds. She even learned how to gut a fish properly, which was less disgusting to do than it looked, and worth it once the fish was done and she took the first tender bite.

Diamond was delighted to have someone to teach. He was so full of knowledge about the seaside that Rose asked him one day if he'd grown up on the coast.

"No," he said, looking out to sea. "I was hatched in Tirras and didn't see the ocean until I was grown. But I love it here, and if you love something dearly, you learn all about it."

By the end of the first week, Rose felt more competent than she ever had before. She understood Diamond's obsession with fishing and spent hours on the wing with him, hunting for specific types of fish.

In between fishing, cooking, and eating, she painted. She had brought several canvases and filled them with seascapes, including one featuring Diamond flying in the distance. When a storm blew through one afternoon, Rose rushed out to stand between the dunes so she could see what the ocean looked like in rain. She returned to the hut drenched and elated.

"You could have been struck by lightning!" Robin said.

"But I wasn't," Rose said, and the next day she painted the stormy sea.

Rose caught her first bluetail at the end of the week, entirely by herself, although it wasn't as big as the one Diamond had caught their first day. She cooked it herself too, from starting the fire to deciding when it was done. Everyone declared it was the sweetest fish they'd ever eaten.

After they'd reduced the carcass to a head and tail and a lot of thin bones, Robin struck a triumphant pose. "Ladies!" she announced in her actor's carrying voice. "It's time for a celebration."

Rose was slower on the uptake than Crystal, who shouted, "A celebration!"

"Of what?" Rose asked.

"Our egg months are over!" Robin leaped into the loose sand above the high tide mark and started a silly little dance. "It's time to take a new lover," she sang. "It's time to fuck a new lover!" She switched her tail back and forth in the sand, leaving a track that looked like strange writing.

Crystal and Rose joined her, laughing, and they danced in a circle for several minutes. The males watched them eagerly.

Rose caught Flame's eye and gave a flirty toss of her head. The sun was setting over the ocean, bathing everything in deep pinky-orange light as though the sea itself was turning royal red.

They collapsed on the sand finally, giggling. Rose wriggled onto her back, paws in the air, enjoying the feel of sand scrubbing her hide. She lifted her head to see if Flame was watching her—he was, of course—and noticed movement in the air.

A dark-colored dragon soared toward them. This intrusion by a stranger felt dangerous and Rose sat up, shaking sand from her wings. The others looked up too.

"It's Evergreen," Crystal said, sounding surprised. Diamond gave her a sharp look and Rose wondered if he had hoped to mate with her.

Evergreen thumped to the sand nearby, panting audibly. "I've done it!" he said, his voice shrill with excitement.

"Done what?" Flame asked, barely glancing at him.

"I'm free at last!"

Rose exchanged a puzzled glance with Robin. She felt something was wrong beyond her general dislike of Evergreen. His voice sounded strange, nervous and exultant at the same time.

Elm stood and made a show of snapping his wings open and refolding them neatly. "I can't stay. In fact, I left at least an hour ago." He leaped into the air and coasted toward the hut.

Diamond stood too. "I went fishing, of course. I'm sorry to have missed Elm." He sounded his old self, his banker self. He took off too, flapping out to sea rapidly.

Crystal slapped the sand with her wings like an angry child. "How could you?" she said, gasping with emotion. "You monster, it was only ever supposed to be a joke!" She scrambled into the air and flew after Elm. Robin, looking startled and alarmed, followed.

Rose glanced at the only other dragon left, Flame. She had a terrible feeling she knew what had happened. From Flame's expression, he knew too.

Evergreen said peevishly, "Why is everyone so stupid? This is ridiculous. Rose, you know it's ridiculous, right? You had to put up with her too!"

Rose mantled her wings and bared her teeth. She thought of Beryl staring into the pond for hours, posing for a gift for a family who hated her.

Flame stalked forward, his wings mantled too and his head down. "Get out. Leave now."

"I just got here. I'm tired."

"Then walk into the sea and be done with you." Flame's voice was a snarl.

"Steady on!" Evergreen backed away as Flame advanced. "What's got into everyone, anyway?"

"Go!" Flame leaped at him.

The two dragons tussled, a confusing tangle of wings and limbs. Rose's heart raced as though she too were about to fight. She saw the flash of teeth in the fading sunset and Evergreen flinched away. A moment later he was running up the beach, followed closely by Flame, and then the two jumped into the air and the pursuit disappeared over the dunes.

Rose stayed where she was, trying to hear voices or wingbeats over the surf and her own blood in her ears. Eventually she sat down in the sand.

She should leave too. She could reach the nearest village in only a few hours.

It felt like ages before Flame returned, although the sun still glowed red on the horizon like the last coal in a fire pit. He landed lightly nearby.

"Are you all right?" Rose could barely see more than his outline in the increasing gloom.

"Just a few scratches. Evergreen won't bother us again."

Rose wondered what had happened and decided she didn't want to know.

She lay down and dug her claws into the sand. "We were all so happy and now it's ruined. I don't know what to do."

Flame approached slowly, as though he was uncertain too. "Things will be clearer in the morning."

"Will Elm really leave?"

"I saw him flying inland with Robin and Crystal."

Rose knew she could catch up with them if she started soon. But she didn't want to leave, not yet. She found a piece of shell and turned it over in her fingers, then dropped it again when Flame stood over her.

He smelled of blood and musk and was still breathing hard from the fight. He looked down at her, his expression invisible in the darkness.

Rose breathed his scent deeply. She realized she'd rolled over without intending to, baring her belly and vent.

He settled across her—cautiously, as though afraid she would change her mind. Rose wrapped her wings around him and pulled him closer.

"You sure?" he whispered.

"Yes." Rose wanted to explain that this, at least, was one thing she understood: the body's age-old demand, as important as food and water and sleep. Instead she just rubbed her muzzle along his throat and opened her vent to him.

Twenty

Rose and Flame slept on the beach, huddled together for warmth. Rose woke first and peeked out from under his wing in the gray pre-dawn light.

The sky was clear, still full of stars. Little pale crabs scurried up and down the sand and the first birds were calling. It would be a good morning to fish.

With a wave of sadness, Rose realized she wouldn't be fishing today. It was time to visit Oriole Sky.

She wriggled out from under the sleeping Flame, got a drink from the nearby stream, and walked down the beach to the hut. She entered as quietly as possible but Diamond said, "Who's there?"

"Just me," Rose said. "I need to pack my things."

"I'm sorry you can't stay."

"So am I. You're staying, right?"

"Yes." Rose heard Diamond turn over in the darkness. "You and Flame?"

He sounded diffident and Rose suspected he'd seen them together when he returned from his night flight. "Just a dalliance," she said, shaking sand out of her blanket.

Rose only stopped once, in the foothills, to refill her water skin at a stream and eat a few rice cakes she'd brought with her. Then she continued, determined to reach Tirras by lunchtime.

She didn't quite manage it, but it was still only early afternoon when she landed in front of the Sunny Garden Gallery. She peeked in through one round window to make sure no customers were there before she went in.

Dawn said, "I didn't realize you'd be back so soon. How was Oriole?"

"I haven't been yet. I'm leaving now, for good, and I have a few things to clear up. Will you go through all my canvases and decide what you want to sell and what I should gesso over?"

Dawn had never visited Rose's lodging house and she felt awkward, later, showing her and her sons inside. She'd already cleaned the room as much as possible, leaving only the dozen or so paintings she'd finished but wasn't certain about. She added the new seascapes, which were still wet.

Dawn liked the seascapes, especially the stormy one, and turned down a few Rose knew weren't very good. Then she came to the ones Rose thought of as "messy," the fast-and-loose style she kept returning to when she had time.

"Why didn't you show this to me before?" Dawn pointed at the new year's race painting, the one that was mostly wings.

"It's so different from the others."

"It's better! And this one. All of these." Dawn stared at the newspaper seller piece, then turned to look directly at Rose. As always, her voice was steady and calm, but Rose read emotion in it too. "This is what you need to focus on. Paint from the gut, Rose, not from the head. Your other work is pretty, sometimes brilliant, but this is *art*."

"Can you sell it?"

"Yes, but I won't. It pains me to say this, but you need to send these pieces home to sell later. I'll pack them up and arrange the shipment for you."

"Thanks." Rose rubbed her face with both paws. "I should take one to show Oriole."

"Show her by painting a new one when you get there."

Oriole had sent Rose directions to her home, which was several hours' flight from Tirras, deep in the mountains. Rose slept one last night in her bare room, turned in the key, and left Tirras early in the morning.

"I'm never coming back," she told herself as she circled endlessly to gain height. The city grew smaller and smaller below her, until it was nothing but a geometric pattern spilled across the mountains' knees. The valley beyond looked like a big green plate with a silvery crack across it, the river reflecting the sky.

In her letter, Oriole had suggested Rose fly through a well-known gap in the mountains east of town. Rose had examined her map carefully that morning, compared it to Oriole's directions, and decided to go straight over the three tall peaks behind Tirras. She knew it would take her longer to do so than to go around, but she also wanted the experience. Besides, she had never found out why their tops were white.

It took her most of the morning to toil her way up and up through ever thinner and colder air. The fir trees on the mountain slopes gave way to low-growing plants, interspersed with gray rocks. Soon there were hardly any plants at all. The only sound was Rose's own labored breathing and the faint slapping of her wing leathers.

Up close, the mountaintops were enormous, all craggy bare stone and flinty soil where nothing grew. Rose landed on a slab of stone to rest, gasping in a most unhealthy way. She simply could not get enough air.

The whiteness lay like a blanket just above her on the slope, with smaller pockets here and there nearby. She stretched an already cold paw toward the nearest pocket and touched it.

It was bitterly cold and compressed under her finger. When she scooped up a tiny piece of white and brought it to her nostrils, it had no scent. And when her clouded breath met it, it melted into a drop of water.

"It's frozen water!" Rose thought, since she had no breath to spare for talking aloud. "It's like hail but soft."

She marveled at it, squinting at the slope above her. It shone so brightly in the sunshine that the glare hurt her eyes.

Then she took to the sky again, because if she didn't reach richer air soon she would die.

She was able to coast between the peaks and down their far side, barely needing to do more than angle her wings. She was profoundly relieved when her heart stopped banging so fast.

"I have achieved something large and ridiculous," she thought once she was flying normally and the cold no longer made her ache.

She reached Oriole's house only an hour later, more by luck than navigational skill. Oriole had noted that her roof was painted blue, and a spot of blue caught Rose's eye in the distance as she was flying in quite the wrong direction.

It was a large, low house with plenty of windows. Rose noticed some neglected-looking flowerbeds and a carefully-tended vegetable garden as she landed by an arched door.

She folded her wings and knocked.

Twenty-One

Rose had imagined Oriole Sky as a more sophisticated version of Honey. But Oriole, it turned out, was rather homely, her hide a mottled gray and yellow. She greeted Rose warmly, introduced her to her mate Kestrel, and insisted she rest and warm up by a crackling fire. While Rose basked in the heat and felt her overworked muscles unknot, Oriole asked all about Honey. Kestrel brought them bowls of mutton stew.

"You must stay for a while—at least a few days, or longer if you can," Oriole said. She glanced up as Kestrel shuffled into the room carrying a plate. "Oh, sweetheart, is that a cake? Thank you!" She said to Rose, "He's a marvel. He actually likes to cook."

"It's carrot cake," Kestrel said. "Carrots from my own garden." He was a faded gray with patches of pink.

After they ate, Oriole showed Rose her studio. It had big windows on three sides and was rather chilly as a result, but the mountain views more than made up for it. Rose marveled at the views, at Oriole's paints and brushes arranged in perfect tidiness in a huge cabinet, and at the paintings.

"I never can work on just one thing at once," Oriole said. "I'm slow and easily bored. I usually have three or four canvases going at once."

"They're all beautiful," Rose said. She hesitated, unsure how to ask her next question without sounding fawning. "Do you ever get tired of being so *good*? Do you ever wish you had a challenge again?"

Oriole looked startled, then sat back on her haunches and laughed. "Good? Rose, I'm terrible! I paint the same things over and over, because I love the mountains and I can't stop myself, and every time I start a new canvas I think that this time, surely, I'll really capture the heart of why I love them. But I never do."

"But your paintings make me ache, they're so good," Rose said. She wondered if Oriole was teasing her.

"If you paint the same things over and over, you learn to paint them well. But there's a step beyond 'good' that I don't think I'll ever achieve." Oriole went over to the cabinet and took a palette from the cupboard. "Do you want to paint for a bit? I think I want to. Join me if you like; I've got lots of canvases—here, have one."

Rose ended up at an easel next to one of the best artists she'd ever met, with permission to use Oriole's high-quality paints, and stared at the blank canvas in horror.

While Oriole happily puttered with a half-finished canvas, Rose's mind skittered frantically, considering and rejecting potential subjects. Finally, frustrated and tired, she looked out the window and painted the first thing she saw, one of the overgrown flowerbeds.

She had to rough in the background first. The sky was easy, a clear, cloudless blue today. Then the mountains, the tallest of them white-topped, then the trees closer to the house. Rose worked quickly, trying to suggest details in as few strokes or dabs of color as possible.

It wasn't her best work, certainly nothing to send home or try to sell in Tirras. But it wasn't terrible either, just a bit soulless.

"Are you done already?" Oriole glanced at her canvas. "Oh, I love that style! It's full of movement. You've made my failed attempt at gardening into something lovely after all."

Rose looked at Oriole's meticulous, glorious painting of the same view and thought she was being awfully kind. But the praise felt good too.

Rose stayed with Oriole for several weeks. They painted every day, sometimes in the studio and sometimes outside, and Rose allowed her time in Tirras to fade as though it had happened a long time ago.

She only achieved a few canvases she felt were genuinely good. "You're too critical of yourself," Oriole said. Rose wished she could ask Honey for her honest opinion, and started thinking of the return trip home.

She still wanted to visit South Stekka. It was a long flight through the mountains, though, with only a few widely scattered villages on the way. But her guide book said that the city of Sather was worth seeing for the ancient earthworks alone.

Over dinner one evening, Rose asked, "Have either of you visited Sather? I might go there next."

Kestrel said, "The papers say there's unrest in Sather."

Rose thought of Flame for the first time in days. "Is it dangerous?"

"Hard to say. We don't get a lot of news from Sather, it's so remote. But the earthworks are astounding. They're supposed to be burial places for ancient royalty."

That made Rose think of Flame even more, although she didn't want to. "I'd like to see the earthworks. Maybe I'll head south soon."

"Wait until the rain stops," Oriole said. It had been raining all day.

The rain cleared up by morning. Rose was ready to pack her things and go, but Oriole suggested one more day's painting. "The mist is so beautiful in the valleys. We'll fly up to Bright Peak. It's not far."

Bright Peak was one of the mountaintops visible from Oriole's house, not especially tall. Rose agreed that the mist was worth seeing. It pooled in the valleys and hung on the mountains' sides as though a giant had torn a cloud into rags.

Rose brought her travel kit, which was identical to Oriole's. "That must be Honey's. We bought them at the same time," Oriole had said when she first saw it. She sounded wistful. "Skies, that was a long time ago."

Rose landed next to Oriole among a lot of rounded stones and low, prickly bushes. "I can see your house from here," Rose said, unbuckling her kit.

Oriole laughed and started to say something, but broke off almost immediately. "Don't move."

Rose had caught the scent too. "What is it?" It smelled rank, like a filthy dragon, but with a mustiness she associated with birds.

"A ghost hound. It shouldn't bother us; it's rare that they'll attack full-grown dragons. Unless..."

"Unless what?" Rose looked around, trying to spot it.

It slunk out of the nearby undergrowth, larger and faster than Rose had imagined. It was smaller than a dragon but with longer, thinner legs and a skinny tail. Its dull gray hide shone with purple iridescence on its throat; its wings were narrow, its jaws short and powerful. Its dark eyes glittered with animal malice.

"Fly! Rose, fly! Get home, fast as you can!"

The urgency in Oriole's voice, and the fast-approaching hound, made Rose leap into the air before she fully understood what was going on. She flapped hard in a panic, then steadied herself and flew more efficiently. Surely the thing wouldn't chase her long, not once she outdistanced it. But when she glanced over her back, it was actually gaining on her.

Rose's first spurt of alarm turned into terror. She pumped her wings shallowly, rowing herself through the fresh morning air. Another quick glance behind showed that the animal was no longer gaining, but it was still in pursuit.

The blue roof was close now. Rose folded her wings in a swooping dive to the front door, all but crashed into it, and managed to get inside just in time. As she whisked her tail in and slammed the door, it shuddered as the animal threw itself after her.

Rose leaned against the door, whimpering and shaking. She imagined the ghost hound smashing through a window.

Kestrel hurried out from the kitchen. "What's wrong? Are you hurt?"

"Ghost hound," Rose gasped, her teeth all but chattering. "Oriole—she's still out there!"

"It won't hurt her," Kestrel said soothingly. "Go into the kitchen and put the kettle on. I'll chase the hound off."

"But it might kill you! It might go back and kill Oriole!"

"Oh no, it won't bother either of us. They're only aggressive to—well, they used to call them egg hounds. They only attack dragons who are carrying an egg."

Rose's shock that she was growing an egg was almost as great as her shock over the ghost hound. She continued to shake long after Kestrel and Oriole assured her the animal was gone, and felt cold even though she was sitting on the hearth of the great stone fireplace.

"Ghost hounds are quite rare, even in the mountains," Oriole said, pouring Rose more tea.

"It was so fast." Rose wrapped her paws around the warm bowl. Oriole's dishes were thick brown-glazed clay.

"Only over short distances," Oriole said. "Still, if you want to avoid the mountains there's a more or less direct route west to the coast. Ghost hounds only live in higher elevations. If you travel down the coast you'll find more villages to stop at anyway, even though it will take you longer to reach Sather."

Rose realized Oriole assumed she still wanted to travel. The thought of setting foot outside the house at all filled Rose with fear. She wasn't sure how she would get back to Tirras, where she would be safe with other dragons all around her.

Kestrel said, "It sounds rather nice, really, traveling along the coast. Didn't you say you know how to fish, Rose?" He turned to his mate. "We should do some traveling one of these days."

Oriole chuckled. "You'd last approximately one day without a full kitchen. How do you cook the fish?" she asked Rose.

"On a bed of coals, for the thicker ones," Rose said, remembering how the ghost hound's black eyes had glittered. "Smaller ones you can grill on sticks over a fire."

"Aren't they bland?" Kestrel asked. "Oh, I suppose they're salted naturally."

"Yes, most have a good salty flavor and they take on more flavor from the smoke." Rose wished she could go back in time to that night on the beach. She should have refused Flame. She should have flown after Diamond and spent the following week fishing with him.

She sipped her tea. The past was done. She couldn't change it. She had forgotten to register her mating before she left Tirras, but it had been about three weeks ago. That meant she still had over two months until her egg was ready to be laid. She could travel to South Stekka, leave her egg at the hatchery in Sather, and either return home or continue her journey south. Either way, she would avoid the mountains and that would be that.

Oriole and Kestrel were talking about different ways of cooking fish. Rose got up long enough to retrieve her map and guide book.

In the morning, she left Oriole's home and flew west toward the distant coast.

Twenty-Two

Traveling along the coast proved to be thoroughly satisfying. Rose didn't hurry, sometimes spending days at a time in an isolated inlet or bay, fishing and exploring. The days were hot, the nights mild and breezy. She didn't paint at all.

The seaside villages so seldom had visitors that Rose's arrival always prompted a gathering. At first she found this disconcerting, but soon she expected it and made sure to arrive with a good-sized fish dangling from her claws. The villages were so tiny and remote that they seldom did much trading. Her money was no great help to the villagers, but a freshly caught fish was a gift everyone appreciated.

After a few weeks she noticed a change in the way she was treated. When she arrived in a new town, the women of the village would immediately offer her a bowl of juice and insist she rest in the shade. She was growing round as her egg developed, and was touched that strangers worried she might be overexerting herself.

Sather lay along a river delta. It was a swampy area with some homes built on stilts and some on big rafts floating in the vast, sluggish river. The more prosperous homes were inland, built on artificial flat-topped hills.

Rose arrived in mid-morning after a leisurely flight from the nearest village, where she had stayed the night in an actual inn. The inn was full of Satherians vacationing outside of the city, who all told her the city had lost its collective mind. "It's those royalists," one man said with disgust, over orange juice and fish grilled with coconut.

"What do the royalists want?"

"What does anyone want? More power," the man said, and opened his newspaper with an angry snap.

The city looked calm from the air, at least. Rose decided to tour the earthworks first, then find a comfortable lodging house near the hatchery where she could stay until it was time to lay her egg.

Whenever she thought of laying her egg, she wished she had chosen to fly back to Dayrill instead of to Sather. She wanted Honey and her other friends nearby. She wanted home.

"You're here," she told herself, soaring over the great mud-colored river. "You might as well see the earthworks."

The earthworks were famous and there were plenty of signs to guide tourists to see them. They were flat-topped mounds like the ones where houses stood in the city itself, but far larger, built on slightly higher ground a few leagues from the river, with the eager jungle plants kept pruned back.

As Rose coasted down to land, she was surprised at how busy the place was. Hundreds of dragons were rushing about, with more arriving in droves. She wondered if she'd arrived on a holiday or if today was a special school outing.

But as soon as she landed, she realized something had to be wrong. Everyone had the same frantic expression, and everyone seemed determined to enter the earthworks through entrances already clogged with visitors. She saw one man lugging a broken piece of stone, only to be swarmed by five or six others who all tussled to take it from him. Somewhere nearby she heard a crash and turned to see a sign fall over. It read, "This area is the sacred burial place of ancient priest-kings. Please respect our ancestors with silence and reverence."

She skirted the edges of the clearing, hoping to find someone to explain what was going on. The most eerie thing was the silence—as though people had taken the sign's directive to heart. Despite the hundreds of dragons around, no one spoke. The drone and chime of insects in the trees was far louder, a constant sound she barely noticed after a few minutes.

She saw a low fence ahead, broken in places. A structure that had once stood on a big dais within the fence now lay scattered on the ground. Dragons pawed through the pieces as though searching for something. Rose heard a man pleading with them to stop.

She headed for the voice. As she did, she stepped over broken pieces of the structure and realized they were bones.

"What's happening?" Rose asked. The man had the gawky look of a half-grown dragon although he was an adult. His eyes were wide with alarm and he kept saying, "Please don't. It's only nature—nothing religious. Please leave it alone."

He scooped up a fallen tooth the size of his paw and hugged it to his chest. "You've arrived at a bad time," he told Rose.

"Yes, but what precisely is going *on*?"

"The city has fallen." The man's voice wobbled. "The priests are dead and the royal family reinstated. Please don't. It's not a religious installation," he said to a woman who was trying to break a thigh bone almost as long as her own body.

"I don't understand," Rose said. The woman gave up and bounded past her toward the nearest earthworks, sending some finger bones spinning away. Rose picked them up and offered them to the man.

"Thank you. It's terrible. All my work is ruined. This was a nearly complete skeleton of one of our ancient ancestors, on display for people to learn from. It was found in the mountains and carefully preserved for study."

Rose looked at the bones with more interest. "Dragons must have been enormous in the olden days."

"Yes, but this was much longer ago than even ancient history. We think it might even have lived a million years ago!" His voice held awe mixed with anxiety. Rose couldn't imagine that the world was a million years old.

"This is what we think it looked like when alive." The man righted a fallen sign, dropping the finger bones in the process. He gathered them up again.

The sign showed a clean ink drawing of the skeleton, then a painting that was much less inspiring. The dragon ancestor in the painting was a muddy brown in color and skinny in all the wrong places. Instead of wings it had a second pair of arms.

"How did its arms turn into our wings?" Rose asked.

"Slow changes over many generations. We have even older skeletons where all the limbs are the same length, used for crawling, but you can see that this one's are longer. They might have been used for display."

"It was certainly too big to fly."

"It might have been able to glide short distances. Its bones were lighter than they look, quite like our own bones, but its time in the earth turned them to stone. It had the same breathing system we do and it used that efficient breathing system for *something*." The man brightened with enthusiasm as he spoke, then reverted to worry when someone grabbed a vertebra and lugged it away.

Rose bounded after the man and grabbed the vertebra back. He continued toward the earthworks without a second look at her.

"What are they all after?" Rose asked.

"Knowledge. The priests claimed no one would be reborn in the egg without the secret rites. Now the priests are dead and everyone thinks they'll learn about the rites here." He sounded sad. "There are no secret rites. There are only dragons, behaving as we have since the world began. We hatch, we grow, we mate, we lay eggs, and one day we die and our children carry on the tradition." He cradled the bones and watched the near-silent scramble taking place all around.

Rose glanced back at her round sides. "I was going to leave my egg in Sather's nursery," she said. "I'd better return to Tirras after all."

"I've heard they have their own royalist movement in Tirras, led by a dragon called the Flame King."

Rose felt her claws bite into the hard-packed dirt. "Yes. I know."

More dragons were arriving all the time and the fight to get into the earthworks was intensifying. Rose heard cries of anger and pain that made her shudder. "I think I'd better leave," she said. "You should too."

The man was gathering up all the smallest bones and tucking them into an already stuffed-full bag. Rose helped. He said, "I should be home with my mate and our daughter. I just hoped I could talk reason to the people here."

More fights were breaking out around them. Rose mantled her wings. "I don't think they'll listen to reason."

A dragon landed in the middle of the scattered bones and immediately grabbed one. Five or six dragons attacked him at once and just as suddenly, everyone was fighting. Even before Rose realized consciously what was happening, she launched herself into the air and was winging away toward the river.

The bonekeeper had done the same. "You had better come home with me," he called to her.

Rose was glad to have a safe destination and followed the man closely. There were so many dragons in the air now, all headed for the earthworks, that it reminded her of Tirras.

Twenty-Three

The bonekeeper was named Fern; his mate, who met them on the porch of their small home, was Petal. Petal carried a soft bag with her infant daughter peering out of it.

Rose was captivated by the child, who was a beautiful clear yellow. "She's a fosterling," Petal explained. "There's been such unrest lately that the hatchery is overwhelmed. It put out a general call for foster families and we decided to sign up."

Rose waggled her fingers to make the child laugh. "She must be from the breeding program, she's so beautiful."

"Breeding program?" Petal sounded mystified.

Rose glanced up, surprised. "Don't you have one here?"

Fern said, "I've never heard of such a thing. Who would run it and what would they be breeding for?"

"The city runs it," Rose said. "Whitefall, I mean, where I live. In Dayrill. It's just for,...breeding capable dragons. Attractive and intelligent." The more she spoke, the more uncomfortable she became.

"It sounds like something those awful royalists would come up with," Petal said.

"We don't have a royalist movement in Dayrill. We're quite peaceful."

"So were we, until recently," Fern said.

Rose thought of Flame playing the part of a revolutionary. Maybe he wasn't playing after all.

Petal said, "Anyway, I hope you stay with us for a few days—or longer if you need to. How soon before you lay your egg?"

"About three weeks. I'd better turn back to Tirras." Rose thought of Flame again, thought of the frantic dragons fighting at the earthworks, and lastly thought of home with a longing so fierce it almost overwhelmed her.

Fern said, "Stay overnight, at least. We'll invite a few people over and have a party."

Their house was one of several attached to a big floating dock, although the houses were on stilts in the water. The families were all friends with one another, and Rose got the impression that impromptu parties were frequent occurrences. She helped Fern and Petal prepare their contribution to the meal, a huge pot of fish stew.

As the long summer day ended, the families gathered on the dock to eat together. Rose loaded her plate with a bit of everything to sample, then sat on the edge of the dock with her tail in the water to eat. Rice was a staple here but was a different variety from that grown in Tirras, and the foods were more highly spiced. It made a nice change from her diet the last few weeks, of plain fish and raw fruit.

The talk, of course, was about the royalists. The evening papers were full of terrible news: politicians and priests murdered, people crushed to death at the earthworks. The hatchery had doubled their guards and no one except expectant parents, foster families, and hatchery workers were allowed within the perimeter.

"It sounds terrifying," Rose said to a woman whose name she had already forgotten.

"It is, but I was talking to my grandmother earlier today and she remembers something similar happening when she was still in school. That was when the priests became a central power, although it seems peculiar to think they weren't always." The woman shrugged her wings. "She said it was turmoil for a long time, but everyone soon became used to it and went about their lives."

Rose thought, *I'm not staying here one second longer than necessary*, but she only said, "I suppose people can get used to anything, even quite horrid things."

"It's too bad we have to. But dragons are resilient."

Another woman nearby, whose two children who kept jumping in and out of the river to swim, said, "I don't intend to let my chicks get used to horrid things. I've spent all day packing up necessities to leave. I'll give the rest to charity."

"Where are you going?" the first woman asked.

"To stay with my sister in Avva. She says the school there is first rate."

Someone else chimed in, "I've heard the Avvan dramatics program is quite good."

For a few refreshing minutes, the talk turned to school programs and then to the activities of the various families' children. Rose accepted a bowl of orange juice someone brought her and let herself relax.

It was a beautiful night. The half-moon rode high in a starry sky and the riverbanks glittered with millions of fireflies—more than Rose had ever seen in one place. She heard music and laughter in the distance from other gatherings, saw young dragons swimming or flying low over the water to fish. She even saw someone sitting on a wooden raft, pushing it along with a flat piece of wood. The sight was so astonishing that she stared until the figure was hidden behind nearby homes.

Rose was safe among friendly dragons, with good food and a place to sleep. The world felt untroubled. She wished it were.

Rose dreamt she laid her egg in the stone ribcage of a giant ancestral dragon, but that a silent mass of pushing, shoving dragons rushed through and scattered the bones. Her egg was kicked here and there by unheeding paws, rolling about while Rose scrambled after it in desperation. She woke with her heart pounding.

Petal was already up, eating fried rice cakes for breakfast and feeding her daughter tiny bites. She greeted Rose when she came into the kitchen. Outside the window, a dozen brightly colored ducks floated on the water, preening their feathers.

"Fern's already gone for the day. He and his colleagues are going to see if they can rescue some of the bones."

Rose had only just shaken off her dream. She wrapped her wings around her body as though that would protect the egg she carried. "I hope he's all right. It was terrifying yesterday."

"I told him to fly away if he felt even the least bit in danger." Her daughter opened her mouth wide and Petal set a small amount of rice on the girl's tongue. "I know his work is important, and that dragonkind would benefit from knowing more about our distant ancestors, but living dragons are even more important. Especially his daughter. And me." Petal's voice faltered, and Rose realized her calm demeanor must hide a great deal of fear.

"Will you stay here?" Rose asked.

"Maybe. The morning papers are full of warnings, but it's hard to tell what's exaggeration."

"I'm going back to Tirras before my egg is ready to be laid."

"I don't blame you," Petal said sadly. "Once things settle down here, I do hope you come back. It's wonderful here, you have no idea. This isn't the right time of year to visit—it's too hot and there are too many flies. Once the weather cools down in autumn we have festivals I don't think you'll find anywhere else." Petal set her bowl down so she could gesture with her paws. "All the musicians play—so much music everywhere, and dancers, and all sorts of fun things to do and see. Have you heard of the Night Dancers? They dress up as beasts and go about in groups, dancing and performing funny plays. It's marvelous! Oh, I hope things go back to normal soon."

Her daughter opened her jaws and made an impatient "ah, ah!" sound. Petal gave her another bit of rice.

"Anyway," Petal said in a more measured voice, "Help yourself to some cakes, and there's fruit over by the stove. Will you stay here today?"

Something alarmed the ducks and they all took off together, their wingbeats loud in the quiet morning. "No, thank you. I want to get an early start."

Twenty-Four

After consulting Petal and her guide book, Rose decided to return to Tirras through the mountains. Time was against her and home was constantly in her thoughts now. She didn't say so to Petal, but she wanted to lay her egg not in Tirras, but at *home*.

She left Sather with relief and flew inland, keeping the river in sight until she saw mountains blue in the distance. The river was dotted with tiny communities and when she grew tired, she stopped at one for juice or fresh fruit. No one in South Stekka drank plain water, she'd noticed, and tea was similarly rare. But the country was so warm and lush, she supposed fruit grew year-round.

She stayed the night in a tiny town and left the river behind the next morning. The land grew rumpled like the edge of a blanket, then gave way quite suddenly to mountains. They were steep but not white-peaked, and indeed some had odd flat tops crowned with jungles. She passed one waterfall so tall that the wind caught the water halfway down and scattered it like rain.

She was delighted to see a village on one of the flat-topped mountains just when she was hungry for lunch. As she glided closer, she noticed a great many new houses around the village's edge, small and roughly built. When she landed, a dozen people rushed up to ask her for the latest news from Sather. Half the villagers were people who had fled Sather weeks before.

The village's only restaurant was a bigger version of the local houses, which were rounded with thatched roofs. Instead of doors and windows, they had walls that could be rolled up and tied open to catch the breeze.

The restaurant tables were communal, with people dropping in and out all the time. Some people paid with freshly killed meat or freshly picked vegetables instead of coins. Rose ate roast wild piglet and fried plantains, which were smooth and lightly sweet, with slices of melon to slake her thirst.

An older woman with a malformed wing sat down across from Rose. "It's good to see a new face," she said. Rose had trouble understanding her thick accent. "Lots of people from Sather, not so many from anywhere else these days."

"I'm heading home to Dayrill to lay my egg there."

The woman surveyed Rose's round sides. "Eh, better hurry." She laughed. "I've had five eggs myself."

"Five! That's wonderful." Rose hesitated, unsure whether she should bring up an unpleasant topic over a meal. "You don't have ghost hounds here?"

"Eh?"

"Ghost hounds. You know, egg hounds?"

"Oh, them." The woman made a dismissive "poof" sound. "Just bite them. They're not strong. Go snap-snap-snap and scare them off, like so." She stood up and pounced at an imaginary enemy, her teeth gnashing and her good wing mantled. Then she sat back down with a self-satisfied air.

"They still scare me," Rose admitted.

"You're strong enough to carry your egg through the mountains and home. You're stronger than any hound."

Rose took comfort from the woman's words, but when she left after her meal she still took care to fly high above the mountains, just in case.

For the next week Rose flew through the mountains, which grew taller and less jungly as she traveled. The towns were widely spread but not too far to fly between in a day, and there were plenty of rooms in the various inns and taverns.

"No one's traveling to Sather right now," one restaurant server told her. "Our whole town depends on the tourist trade. I hope Sather rights itself soon."

That night Rose was delighted to be served tea with her meal, her first in weeks. She savored the fragrant steam that rose from her bowl as much as the taste.

She had arrived in town fairly early and spent the evening exploring before it got too dark. There wasn't much to the village, but it was quaint and she enjoyed poking through its small shops.

When she returned to the hotel, she ordered a pot of tea and biscuits and ate them on a tiny balcony overlooking the town. The night was mild and breezy, promising rain overnight. Rose felt surprisingly content.

She had more tea with breakfast, lingering over the meal as long as possible. The night's rain had settled into a drizzly morning. She didn't want to fly in the rain, but a day's delay might mean laying her egg in a city where she knew no one.

She kept thinking of Petal's daughter, of small Rose. At some point she realized she intended to keep her egg instead of leaving it at a hatchery.

"Very well," she thought. "Honey won't mind and the child might even grow up to be an artist."

The clouds broke up by mid-morning. Rose left immediately, even before the rain had fully stopped. It was only patchy, though, and the sun shone through and scattered rainbows about. Rose flew fast, hoping to arrive at the next town long before nightfall. It was her last stop before Tirras.

She arrived at dusk and coasted down to a sizeable city. Prices were high this close to Tirras, and although she had plenty of money with her, Rose visited several inns before she found one she considered reasonably priced. She took her pack off with relief and left it in her room, then went to find a restaurant.

She was tired of traveling. She was tired in general. She wanted her own room at home, her friends and colleagues within earshot if she needed something. She even wanted meals prepared by indifferent cooks who kept getting distracted by art.

She wondered if she would discover, once she arrived home, that she was dissatisfied with Whitefall after all. Certainly she thought differently about its breeding program now, and would undoubtedly notice the disparity between rich and poor in a way she never had before. She might even grow weary of the streets she knew so well.

"It's no use thinking it'll be just the same," she said aloud. She was walking on a dirt path that ran behind some buildings on one side, thick fir trees on the other. No one was around to hear her talk to herself. "You've changed, even if you didn't want to. That's the point of traveling. If you're dissatisfied with home, you'll have to learn what you want and how to get it."

For some reason she thought of Sable. Instead of being embarrassed by her thoughts, she laughed aloud. Maybe it was time she found a mate. She and Sable got along.

This line of thought was so interesting that she didn't notice the ghost hound until it was nearly upon her.

It was bigger than the one she'd seen with Oriole, patterned silver and black. As it bounded toward her, Rose's terror blazed into a fury unlike any she had ever felt.

She would not let it have her egg. She leaped at it, her jaws open. Its rank, bird-like smell filled her nostrils.

Instead of fighting back, the ghost hound scrambled away. Rose pursued it into the trees. Just before it got its wings open to fly, she caught it by the tail. A moment later she locked her teeth in its throat and bit its life out as though it were a fish.

In only a minute or so it lay still. Rose had not realized its hide was feathered until she was spitting tiny feathers out of her mouth.

"Ugh. I'll never get the taste out," Rose said aloud. She was shaking—but she was triumphant too. She left the body and hurried toward the nearby buildings.

She spent the rest of the evening drinking tea and eating a great many iced buns. She felt she deserved them.

Twenty-Five

It felt surreal to land in front of the Sunny Garden Gallery as though no time had passed.

Rose entered the gallery and Dawn gave her a startled look. "Skies! You look like you're going to lay your egg right now."

Rose laughed. "I have about two weeks left, I think. I only stopped by to collect any money you might have for me. I'm heading home."

"After you've laid your egg, surely."

"I don't really want my baby growing up in Tirras. Sorry."

"No, I understand. But it's only worse here because Tirras is so large. There's rich and poor in every city. If you don't see the poor ones, it's because you're not looking."

Rose thought of home. Whitefall had seemed so large to her once. "Have you ever laid an egg?"

"No. I don't really like mating with males. My fosterlings are the world to me, though."

"How are they doing?"

They talked for a while, about Dawn's boys, small Rose and her family—Dawn had helped Briar find a better job—and volunteer work. Then Dawn wrote out an account of the money owed to Rose and signed it. "Better take this to the bank right away. You don't want to lose it."

"I'll do that now. Thanks for everything, Dawn. Come visit me one day."

When Rose entered the big bank where Diamond worked, he looked as startled to see her as Dawn had. Rose nodded to him. "I need to deposit this. How have you been?"

"Good. You look...round."

Rose almost laughed, except that the hushed bank interior wasn't the place for laughter. "Thanks for teaching me to fish. I traveled down the coast all the way to Sather, fishing as I went."

"That sounds brilliant." Diamond looked envious. "Will you be around tonight? We're seeing a show."

"No, I'm leaving as soon as I'm done here. I'm going home."

Diamond wrote the new, much larger total at the bottom of her letter of credit and stamped it. "I know Flame would like to see you. Will you visit him if I give you his address?"

Rose considered it—but what did she have to say to Flame? She could tell him about the turmoil in Sather, but he wouldn't understand the horror. He would only explain how he would do things better in Tirras.

"No," she said to Diamond, and left.

Rose flew across the great Tirras valley that day but didn't try to travel any farther. She stopped at the far end of the valley and spent the night at an inn. As her guide book promised, the locals were friendly and the prices reasonable.

Her flight through the foothills was uneventful and by the following evening she had left the mountains far behind. She spent the night at another inn and consulted her map while she ate breakfast the next morning.

She was nearing Elkton. How long would it take her to reach home from there? Four days, maybe three if she found a tailwind.

Her map indicated which cities had hatcheries. There were more than she'd expected and many were an easy day's flight from each other. She could travel from city to city in case her egg came before she made it home, and she might even find time to sight-see a bit in the evenings.

She passed Elkton the next morning without stopping, not without regret. She wanted to check in on her young artist friends.

"I'm not *that* far from home," she said out loud, as Elkton receded behind her. "I can visit whenever I like. I just have to find someone to take my shop day."

The thought of the shop, and her own little bedroom upstairs, nearly overwhelmed her with homesickness. She was weary of traveling, bored of the wide world. She wanted to be *home*.

It took her two days to cross Varrill. She stayed in a city only an hour from Inkle's border the second night. She would certainly be home within two days if she pushed herself—but she wasn't sure she should push herself. Her egg felt as though it was shifting inside her, getting into position to be laid.

She decided to continue toward Rellis, one of the largest cities in Inkle. If she had her egg there, it was close enough to home that she could collect the baby when it hatched. Hatcheries always supplied a soft carry-bag to new mothers, so they could bring their hatchlings home in safety.

How strange to think of bringing home a hatchling, a new life that was even now forming in the egg inside her. No wonder there were so many poems and songs about the marvels of the egg; no wonder Sable's paintings of eggs in peril caused such outrage.

Full of thoughts, with home pulling at her more strongly than ever, Rose ate a quick, light breakfast and took to the air.

The day was sunny, the ground far below mostly patchwork farms and fields. Rose soared on strong thermals, barely needing to flap her wings. She passed over Inkle's flower-flag border and was flying high enough that she couldn't even hear the flocks of sightseers. She did wish she had time to land and have juice and cakes at the picnic grounds near the flags. But she didn't have much of an appetite today anyway.

She felt all right when Rellis came into view on the horizon. It was barely past noon and Rose landed long enough to eliminate, drink some water, and rest in the shade. Should she push on toward home?

She wanted to. She was making such good time riding thermals that she could be home *that night*. She could fly directly to the hatchery in Whitefall, sleep there until her egg came, then go home.

"All right," she said out loud. "Go home, then."

She stood and pulled her pack back on with reluctance. She was sick of carrying it. And when the time came to launch herself into the air again, she felt so heavy and awkward that she had to flap hard to stay aloft until an updraft carried her into the sky.

Her center of gravity had shifted, making her tail-heavy. She remembered her health lessons in school and knew her egg would be ready to lay today. She must have added the dates wrong, or her egg was ready a bit early.

She flew homeward.

Twenty-Six

Rose rowed herself through the sky with shallow, fast wingbeats. When her wings tired, she coasted on the updrafts to rest them.

An hour or so later, her egg pains started.

They were mild at first, an intermittent cramping in her gut as though she'd eaten something that disagreed with her. She reassured herself that many dragons had these mild pains for hours and hours until the egg was ready to lay.

The ground far below seemed barely to move, like bad dreams she'd had as a child where she tried to fly from danger but could only drift like thistledown.

"I'm traveling fast," Rose thought. "I'll be home soon. I'll be home soon." But as her egg pains increased, she found it harder to keep up her pace.

She saw the other Inkle flower flag border in late afternoon, meaning she had crossed the country in a single day. "I am *almost home*," she gasped aloud to herself. "I'm in Dayrill now. I'm only hours from Whitefall."

She forced her tired wings to move faster. Her egg pains were so intense that sometimes she had to stop flapping and coast until a cramp passed.

Still, there was time between each cramp. She had time. She still had time.

The long summer day stretched out endlessly. Rose felt she had been flying without cease for a lifetime. She clenched her innards against her egg's movement. "A few more minutes. I just need a little more time."

Suddenly she recognized the countryside. The patterns of forest and pasture, town and river snapped into focus in her mind. That was Foxbury far below, with the quaint humped bridge she had painted that fateful day so many months ago.

"Just a little more time—less than an hour," she muttered, and put on as much speed as she could manage.

The outskirts of Whitefall came into view. But her egg was insisting that it be laid *now*. Her pains were almost constant and she felt her insides shift to make room for the egg's passage. She imagined the egg falling out of her, falling, falling.

"No!" Rose squeezed her vent muscles despite the pain.

The first of Whitefall's buildings passed by below. The hatchery was close—but home was closer.

She angled her wings into a steep dive, straight at the modest gallery building on Riverside Lane, straight at her own window.

It was open, fortunately. She backwinged hard and pulled her wings in, and shot into the room.

"Honey!" she bellowed. "Anyone—I need help!" She tried to shout again but only mewled as another cramp seized her.

Honey was next to her suddenly. "You'll be all right. Relax. Let the egg come." She added sharply, "Elm, you're not wanted here right now."

"Sorry," Elm said, although Rose could barely hear him over the roar of blood in her ears.

"You too, Sable. I know you're out there."

Sable's voice came from the hallway. "Welcome back, Rose."

Rose's claws bit into the wooden floor. Honey said. "Blossom, put the kettle on for tea and send May up here. Sable, get *out*."

"I was just curious."

Rose heard hasty paws up and down the stairs. Then May was next to her too. "Rose, you really do need to relax."

Blossom bounded into the room. "Skies, Rose, you're big as a house." Her voice was loud and excited, and when Rose looked up through a blur of tears, Blossom appeared sleekly elegant. May and Honey were likewise lovely. How beautiful her friends were! What perfect companions for this important moment.

"It's time to lay your egg." Honey's voice was firm. Rose took a deep breath, stretched out flat on the floor, and let the next cramp push her egg out of her body.

"There, see?" Honey said. "Easy."

"Not really," Rose gasped. She felt her vent was splitting open.

May unbuckled Rose's pack and lifted it off of her. "I put a piece of canvas down to catch the egg, since we don't have a blanket."

Blossom laughed. "The baby will be an artist for certain."

Twenty-Seven

Rose barely remembered the short cart ride to the hatchery, her egg swaddled in blankets and Rose herself curled around it. She barely remembered refusing to leave it.

For the next four weeks, Rose remained at the hatchery with her egg.

When she'd done her hatchery duty as a girl, a woman had refused to leave her egg. Rose remembered feeling embarrassed for her, remembered agreeing with her friends that they would never act so ridiculous.

Now, curled around her egg on its bed of warm sand, Rose sent a silent apology to her memory of the woman. She understood now.

Some ancient instinct had awakened in her, making her unable to leave her egg for even a moment. She eliminated in the sand, covering it tidily and not even caring that the hatchery girls scooped the messes into a pail with barely concealed disgust. She only thought, "They'll understand too one day."

She barely ate. She drank only what she needed to live. She didn't so much sleep as doze constantly, rousing at any noise. And she didn't speak at all.

Males weren't allowed in the hatchery, but Honey, May, and Blossom visited her and brought her favorite foods. Blossom, to Rose's dull surprise, visited her most. She would sit next to Rose for hours, gossiping. From Blossom Rose learned that May had had an egg. "First crack out of the box," Blossom said. "You never saw anyone so smug."

Sometimes Rose suspected that Blossom was making things up in hopes of getting a response from her. "D'you remember that contest one of the papers ran at new year's? Guess how many eggs would be laid and win a chicken every day? Elm entered and won. We've all been eating chicken until it's coming out our ears. May said she's going to put together a cookbook all about how to make chicken a hundred different ways."

Rose got up long enough to turn her egg over carefully, then curled herself around it again. Perhaps Blossom was lonely and wanted someone to talk to. Perhaps she was just shirking her duties at home.

Either way, Rose was glad she was there.

The hatchery girls were ever-present, moving around in pairs and chattering happily. The long, low room housed two rows of ten eggs each, and each egg needed turning every few hours. There were lots of other rooms too, and a vast basement where kettles of water stayed at a simmer. The steam rose and kept the rooms above at just the right temperature and humidity.

Rose had hated stoking the fires. Her favorite task was turning eggs, but that was everyone's favorite task.

A nurse did her rounds periodically too, checking the eggs and making sure Rose ate and drank enough. All the nurses were practical and most spoke to her in a jolly manner. "You'll be a mother in another week. Won't that be nice? Eat up your gruel or you'll waste away to bones."

Despite all the activity, Rose was alone when her egg showed the first crack.

It was dawn, the skylights barely gray. Rose woke, fully alert at the soft sound of movement in her egg. A moment later she heard a grating noise and a tiny crack appeared on the pearly shell.

Rose gasped. She waited, but when there was no more activity she drifted asleep again, only to wake a few minutes later to a determined tapping from within the egg.

Her heart raced. Her child was strong and healthy, hammering its way through the tough shell with its nose. It made her want to laugh, although she also wished she could help. But it was important that the baby accomplish its hatching without help. As the saying went, "Strong shell, strong dragon."

The small noises, interspersed with quiet while the hatchling rested, continued for some time. The light grew brighter, turning the sky from gray to dark blue. More cracks appeared in the egg.

At last, a tiny triangle of shell broke loose and fell to the sand. The hatchling tapped harder and another piece broke, then another. A tiny paw groped awkwardly at the edge of the shell, followed by the entire arm. The shell cracked wide and Rose's child looked up at her blearily.

She put her nose down to the little wet hatchling, its wings folded against its back, and spoke for the first time in a month. "Ember. My son."

Ember was royal red all over with black speckles and streaks. He looked like a living coal pulled from the fire. He fairly glowed in the morning light.

"You are so beautiful," Rose whispered.

He rested against her wing and she carefully sprinkled him with sand, then dusted it off to dry him. He was so tiny to be so perfect. She couldn't look away from him.

A pair of girls came in, both of them yawning. Rose said, "He hatched. His name's Ember. I'm sorry I've been such a bother."

Twenty-Eight

The head nurse gave Rose and Ember a clean bill of health, and Ember ate his first bites of food, the traditional minced grasshopper. Rose was so hungry that she filled out Ember's parentage with a shaking paw. Funny how she hadn't felt hungry all month until now.

The matron said, "Now then, your mate has been waiting patiently for most of the week. He'll be glad to see you."

Rose's heart sank. She didn't want to talk to Flame. He wasn't her mate.

She would spurn him, of course. She had put him down as the father but he had no claim on the child. She would tell him so once they were outside.

Rose tucked Ember into his soft carry bag, awkwardly because she was afraid to hurt him. He was sleeping after his first meal. Although he'd only been out of the egg half an hour, he already seemed bigger. His tiny wings no longer looked crumpled.

Then, carry bag secured around her neck and left arm, she ducked through the leather flaps into the nursery's vestibule, then through the wooden door into the waiting room.

Sable stood up. "Are you all right?"

Rose stared at him. He was the only dragon in the room. He was waiting for her.

"Are you all right?" he repeated. "You've lost weight."

Rose cleared her throat. Her voice was still hoarse from disuse, but there was one important thing she needed to know. "I'm fine. I have a son. Sable, did Elm really win a chicken a day in the newspaper contest?"

They walked home together in the summer sunshine. Halfway there they stopped at a café for tea and iced buns, and Ember had a second meal of a bit of bun crumbled in tea to soften it. Everyone in the café cooed over him.

"He looks like me," Sable said when they resumed their slow walk home.

Rose laughed. Everything was wonderful and she thought she might float away into the sky, she felt so light. "You didn't have anything to do with making him."

Sable rested a wing over her back. "Maybe next time I will."

Before she could respond—or even work out how she felt about his words—he continued, "There's a great big crate waiting for you in the back room, utterly in everyone's way. Honey wouldn't let us open it."

"My paintings," Rose said, surprised. She wondered if she would like any of them when she saw them again.

It was lunchtime when they arrived home. May squealed with excitement when they came into the kitchen, where everyone was eating chicken without enthusiasm. "You're home! Let's see the baby. Oh skies, Rose, he's the most beautiful hatchling I've seen in my life."

Blossom waggled a finger at Ember, who only looked at it. "Not bad, Rose. What color will the next one be, or will you just make it rainbow-colored?"

Honey said, "Have some chicken. In fact, have all the chicken."

"And then you can open your box," Blossom said, "because I keep tripping over it."

Whatever everyone else thought, Rose was sure the chicken casserole was the most delicious food she'd ever eaten. She carefully chewed a mouthful and fed it to Ember, who made his first sound, a happy gurgle. "He likes it," Rose said.

"Spit and all," Blossom said. "Hurry up."

Finally they all gathered in the back room. Elm pried the top off the crate and took out wads of packing straw, then lifted out the first painting and unwrapped it.

It was the new year's race painting. Everyone fell silent, looking at it in the bright light slanting through the window. Rose glanced at Honey to see what she thought.

"It's brilliant," Honey said softly. "Let's see the rest."

One by one Elm unwrapped the paintings and set them against the wall for everyone to examine. It was like school, Rose thought, her heart hammering in her throat, especially her final project where all her classmates and teachers gave critiques and she was certain she'd be denied graduation. But that had turned out well—she'd even sold a few pieces—and this would too.

Her friends gave critiques too. "This is better than anything I could do," Blossom said, her voice raw with envy. Rose tried to protest, but Blossom waved her words away. "I'm not fishing for compliments, I'm being truthful. For once."

Sable said, "It's better than anything I could do too. No, it's different than anything I could do. That doesn't make either of us worse, but your new style is—lively, I want to say."

"Movement," Elm said. "Everything feels like it was moving just a moment ago until you looked, and it froze."

"It's like the sky studies you used to do," May said. "I bought one at your sale, did you know? It's on my wall."

Rose relaxed slowly. And when Honey said, "Whatever you went through during your travels, it was worth it. We'll have to hold a special viewing and sale, of course," she felt she had graduated again.

"This one has a note," Elm said.

Rose looked at the painting in surprise. May said, "That one's different, but it's just lovely! Who is it?"

"A woman named Beryl." Rose read the note.

It was written in Dawn's small, tidy hand. "I thought you might like this so I bought it back from the family. No one wanted it. Beryl had an accident and died while you were away, I'm sad to say. Her grandson is under investigation for possible involvement in her death. I can't say I ever liked him. Write me when you get a chance. Maybe come visit again soon."

Rose read the note twice and the last worried part of her relaxed. Flame hadn't killed Evergreen that terrible night. Ember's father might not be a good person, but he wasn't a murderer.

That evening, Rose took Ember into the courtyard behind the building and stretched out next to him on a blanket. He kept looking at her and trying to focus his eyes.

After a little while Sable came out and said, "May I join you?"

"Of course."

He lay down nearby. "I'm retired from the breeding program, did I tell you? They retire males after twenty offspring. So you have a long way to go to catch up to me."

Rose laughed and said, "The breeding program is an antiquated relic of a stratified society."

"Possibly. It's time for me to concentrate on my art anyway. You've inspired me."

"Will you travel?"

Sable rested his head on his paw, watching her closely. "I don't think so. Are you doing anything tomorrow? Want to go out somewhere?"

Rose said, "I'll have to bring the baby."

"That's fine. Everyone thinks he's mine anyway. It makes me feel important."

They both laughed again. Ember fell asleep against her belly and Rose felt her own eyes grow heavy.

She glanced at the house. In the fading sunset light, she could see an easel propped in every window.

About the Author

Kate Shaw is producer and host of the weekly Strange Animals Podcast, a science-based podcast about living, extinct, and imaginary animals. Her nonfiction book *Beyond Bigfoot & Nessie: Lesser-Known Mystery Animals from Around the World* was published in February 2022. Shaw also writes fantasy and furry fiction as K.C. Shaw. She lives in East Tennessee with her lucky black cats, Dracula and Poe.

You can contact Kate Shaw at kcshaw123@gmail.com.

30501561R00117